Highland Heartbreaker

Highland Hearts
Book 2

Steffy Smith

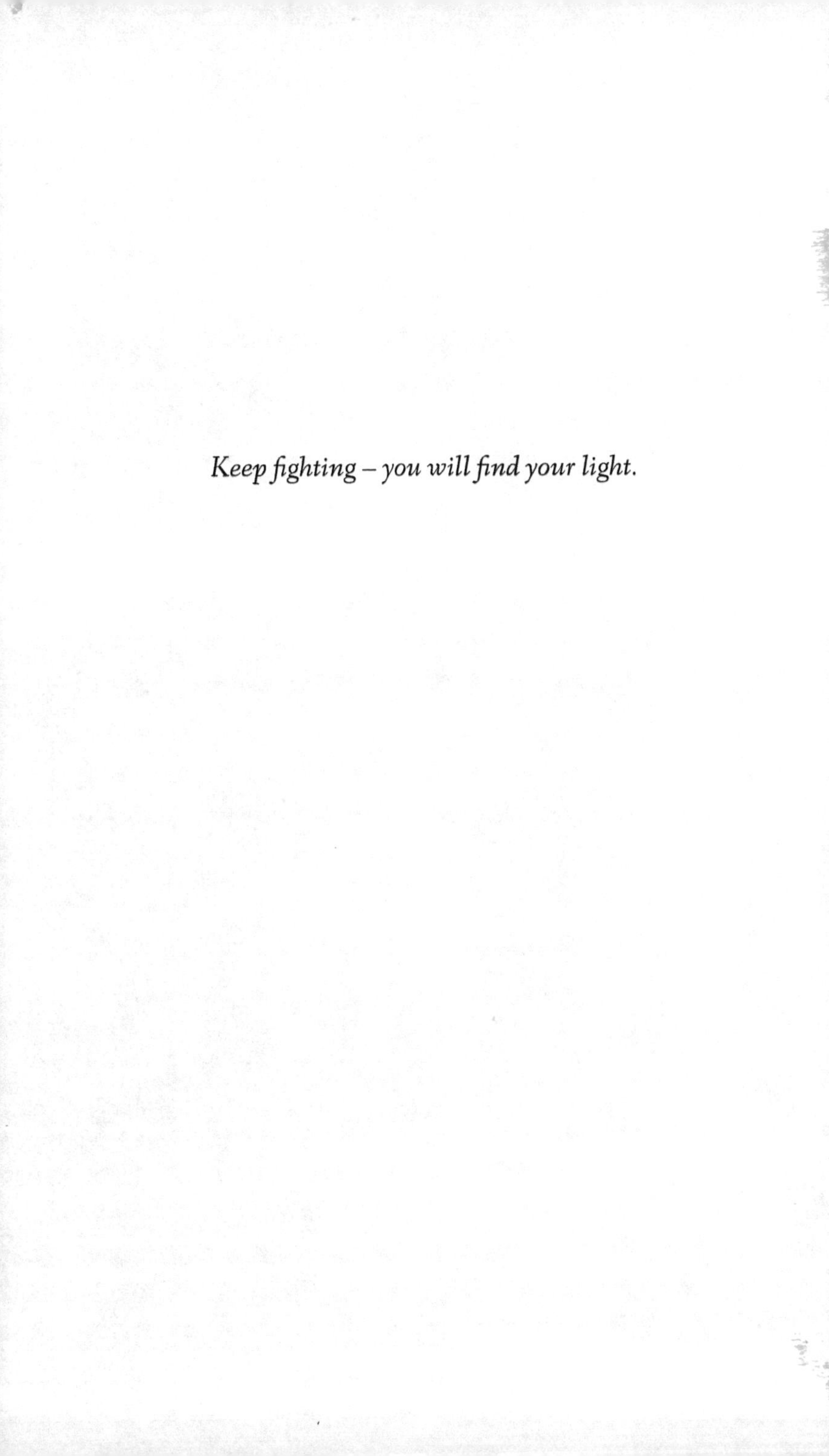

Keep fighting – you will find your light.

Acknowledgement

Ali, Marisa, and Susie – thank you for being sounding boards by way of an appraisal and beta readers. To my editor, Erin, I write this while you are still editing, but I want you to know what a fantastic experience this was!

To all my readers old and new, and the special people who take time to complete advanced reader copy reviews – you all mean the world to me. I love the Historical Romance community, both as a reader and an author. I look forward to sharing more!

Author's Note

I will preface this by reiterating this is a creative work of fiction. Researching history is a favourite pastime and I love being able to take poetic licence regarding real historical figures (who wouldn't want to meet Robert the Bruce) and historical events, like the celebration of Beltane. All the other characters and storyline are purely fictional.

I fervently hope for anyone fluent in Scots Gaelic that I interpreted my translations correctly – always happy for feedback!

Translations

Scots-Gaelic

Bampot ~ idiot
Chan eil mi a 'bruidhinn ach Gàidhlig ~ I only speak Gaelic
Còmhla ri anam ~ soul mate
Each dubh ~ black horse
Feasgar math ~ good evening
Furasta ~ easy
Gàrlach ~ rascal
Is mise ~ my name is
Laochan ~ good lad/friend
Latha Bealltainn ~ Beltane (May Day Festival)
Latha math ~ good day
Leannan ~ sweetheart
Madadh-allaidh ~ wolf
Mo aingeal ~ my angel
Mo chridhe ~ my heart
Mo dhia ~ my god
Mo ghradh ~ my love
Sassenach ~ English person, to a Scot
Seanchaidh ~ storyteller
Seann bhuidseach ~ old witch
Sgian dubh ~ black knife
Tha gràdh agam ort ~ I love you
Tolla-thon ~ arsehole
Uisge beatha ~ water of life/whisky

Words/Phrases (Scottish or otherwise)

Aboot ~ about
Bailey ~ medieval courtyard
Bairn ~ baby/child
Bluidy ~ bloody
Bonnie ~ attractive
Braies ~ pants
Braw ~ attractive (male)
Cannae ~ cannot
Dinnae fash ~ don't worry
Dinnae ken ~ don't know
Haste ye back ~ return back with speed
Ken ~ know
Lad ~ young male
Lass ~ female
Leine ~ shirt
Loch ~ lake
Rood ~ cross/crucifix

Prologue

Scottish Highlands, Murray Lands, 1316

A wizened woman, a *seann bhuidseach* to all that knew her, held up an aged cloth bag to the night sky, asking the powers that be (wherever they may be) to provide blessing for inner sight tonight. A carved Celtic cross gleamed in the Scottish moonlight as an unearthly mist swirled around its height. Her lineage of wise women had passed down magic from the Britons, Romans, Vikings, and her very own Celts, and she embodied it in her own way. Rune casting was one of her favourite crafts.

She cackled as she returned to her lone hut deep in the woods, in front of where the cross stood, knowing her closest companion would be unimpressed with her magic havoc. Gnarled ancient trees, Scots pines, rowans, and hazel trees loomed tall over the solitary hut and all around; no one would even know she was there, unless they knew specifically where to look.

Loki, her companion, a long-limbed black cat, meowed in annoyance, her cackle waking him from his slumber in front of the smoking fire. She waved her hand at him, unperturbed by his protest. Loki tended to find much of what she did annoying, about which she cared nought; they had been together for so long now, she knew he would shortly get over his snit. It was late in the night and there was powerful magic in the air, perfect for rune reading. *I want to embrace every moment of it*, she thought to herself gleefully, as she tossed the first stone.

"Och, Loki, the fates must be in wicked humour as they weave and spin their tales yet to unfold."

At the sound of her voice, Loki stood up and walked over to her, leaping up on a stool to sit beside her at the table. The round wooden tabletop was uneven and littered with herbs, feathers, and flowers spilt from chipped bowls. In front of her, was her set of ancient runes. The wisdom and lore of her ancestors was shared as they had been handed down through many generations. The weathered and worn wood contrasted with the etched symbols which shone brightly, their golden aura enchanting, belying their ancient age. She was bent over so far to eye them, her forehead almost rested upon the table as she stewed over the message being shared.

"*Hagalaz*, the hailstone, the ninth rune. It tells me, Loki, that we need patience and protection; but, who will be needin' to have the patience and who will need protection?" Loki's yellow eyes watched her intently as she brooded over the meaning of this rune with squinted eyes, its message vexing her.

"*Berhana* – this one, Loki, also confounds me." She tapped her chin in concentration as she muttered, "It is nae reversed nor forward, but on its side. This is verra unusual, Loki. Is it telling me of family? I sense new life, but I also sense a loss; but is that loss of the mind, or of the body? Or is it both?"

She moved to the third rune and shook her head, knowing all too well there could be no other interpretation of what the runes represented. And while this last rune gave her no sense of confusion, she felt no joy for what it did represent. A feeling settled within her aged bones – a feeling of dread, despair, anger, and regret. She hovered her hands over the runes and sensed the energy emanating in waves.

"*Ehawaz*. There will be a betrayal," she whispered, tapping her finger on the rune with a symbol displayed like a 'W'.

She stood up, still slightly hunched as her back never straightened, and continued muttering to Loki. "I need to gather more fern, heather, agate, rosemary, apples, elder branches ..."

She rattled off a list of items she needed to replenish her stores, to make spells of protection to assist where needed. Practicality was her nature, not to ruminate over things that cannot be changed. Instead, she prepared for better or worse, until more signs and visions settled upon her. Deciding she did not want to wait for it to happen perchance, she determined to make the magic come to her.

Shuffling over to the fire, she pulled a bowl from a nearby shelf and pinched the contents between her fingers. She spoke clearly into the fire in what can only be described as an ancient language. She threw the dust pinched between her wrinkled fingers into the flickering fire, and the room filled with hazy smoke as she spoke to the other side.

The smoke travelled out the solitary window of the hut, to the Celtic cross, and entwined with the mist. Loki sensed the energy change and the air grow heavy, and lifted a lazy eye to his owner. The woman sat still, her body in the hut but her mind crossed over to another time, as she tried to understand what the future would hold.

Chapter One

Scottish Highlands, MacNichol Lands, 1316

The sound of a heavy drape being sharply pulled back broke through the silence of the bedchamber. The morning light poured in across the stone walls from the Scottish Highland skies, though the colder months this time of year provided a duller glow to the ray of sunlight as it beamed from a grey, muted sky.

"Alex, ye drunken fool, wake up," said a deep, frustrated male voice with a strong brogue.

The warmth on Alexander MacNichol's face welded into his dream-like state, and the voice berating him did not penetrate his ale-induced stupor, so his lusty thoughts continued. *Aye, my bonnie sweet, come lie with me before the fire* – the words played through his mind as he imagined a busty lass with no inhibitions and a saucy grin.

"Och, he smells like he bathed in ale; I am glad I brought extra soap," a husky female voice observed with distaste.

"Aye, *leannan*, ye always come prepared, one of many things I love ye fer."

Alex's erotic dream faded away as these voices started to settle in his mind. *Even in my dreams, I get no bluidy rest. What is this sappy shite I hear buzzing in my head? Maybe if I keep my eyes closed, they will go away.*

"'Tis lucky we got here early, Jamie – I told ye he would need us. He reminds me of a wee bairn sometimes, like he needs someone to watch over him."

"Ye are right, Izzy, *mo chridhe*. But right now, how do we bring him out of the stupor? And please let our bairn tucked in yer belly grow to have more sense than this *bampot*," Jamie replied wryly.

"Let me throw this pitcher of water in his face, that will do the trick," said Izzy in a cheeky tone.

This comment did now penetrate Alex's groggy mind, but before he could yell 'nay', he felt the icy splash of cold water on his face as Izzy dumped the contents of the entire pitcher over his head. He shot up to his feet in an instant, his warrior reflexes engaged.

"By the *rood!*" he yelled. "Why cannae I be left alone?" As he shook his head, the rivulets of water sprang forth in all directions.

"Stop that ye fool, yer flicking water at us. Yer just like Duff after I give him a bath," Jamie scolded him, comparing Alex to his deerhound.

Alex looked up and saw the scowling face of his best friend, Laird Jamie Murray. Beside him stood his diminutive but wise and feisty wife, Lady Isobel Murray, who was staring at him with a slightly bemused, slightly disgusted expression. It was the usual gaze she reserved for him, with of course the one copper eyebrow raised. She was also the bonniest lass in all of Scotland.

Alex looked at his two best friends and ruminated on the journey that brought them together. Izzy healed Jamie from an arrow wound. Jamie took her back to his keep to take care of his sister. Unbeknownst to them both was that Izzy was not a simple village lass, but the daughter of a laird. Alex got to witness firsthand the fiery passion that brought them together and then threatened to tear them apart. He would never forget the look of relief and all-consuming love on Jamie's face when Alex brought her home from her kidnapping. Aye, a love story for the ages theirs was, and now they looked to him for the next.

Mustering a dry tone and an air of dignity only one with his level of arrogance could raise, he threw his head back and straightened his stance. Jamie was the size of a bear, but Alex was slightly bigger and the two of them filled the chamber with their bulk. Highland-born and bred, they had learned everything together: how to ride a horse, how to swing the great claymore with skill, and what it meant to be future lairds. The only difference between them was that Jamie was serious and always looked to do right, and Alex found everything amusing and enjoyed doing anything *not* right. Squaring his feet, Alex faced the two people who had awoken him and attempted to imitate Jamie's stern face.

"Compared to a dog and awoken like a peasant. Pray tell, my dear best friends, what did I do to have ye both grace me with such kind company on this bonnie morn?" Each word was more exaggerated than the last in his deep Scottish brogue.

Izzy slapped him on the arm, her tiny hand surprisingly leaving a sharp sting and he could not help but grin at the little termagant she was.

"Did ye forget ye are to be married today, ye *tolla-thon*?"

asked Izzy, and as usual, not bothering to hide her exasperation.

Alex stared at her blankly, the question hitting him harder than her slap.

"Ye daft fool, she will be here with Robert the Bruce in a few short hours and look at the state of yerself!" exclaimed Jamie, as he looked at Alex's expressionless face.

Aye that is right, 'tis the day of my sentencing, he thought to himself sourly. *And why I decided to wake up alone.*

"I am surprised at ye both, that ye expected to find me waiting with joy fer my bony, whey-faced, miserable English wife," Alex replied in a cranky tone. *Mo dhia, I sound like a mewling babe.*

"I am glad 'tis just ye we have to deal with, and nae ye da as well," said Jamie, shaking his head.

He is right; if there was any time to wed the English, it would be when his da wasnae around.

"Come now, Alex," said Jamie in a gentler tone, at odds with his large stature. "Ye ken this was to happen. Ye may come to enjoy married life! Look at the love I share with *mo aingeal,* Izzy." Jamie's eyes moved to Izzy as he spoke, so he could see the endearing blush that flamed her cheeks when he called her sweet names.

"Well, Jamie, if I had seen Izzy first, trust me – I would have made her mine before ye even had a chance," Alex replied with a roguish wink. How could he let the perfect opening for such a retort pass him by?

"Maybe ye need some more help coming to yer senses this morn?" Jamie asked with a mock fist.

"But, ye wouldn't have tried to wed me, ye would have only tried to bed me, ye rutting beast," Izzy quipped, before Alex riled Jamie up too much. Turning all business, she clapped her hands loudly, causing both men to jump. She smiled at the sight.

"Down to the loch, both of ye. Take the soap, Jamie, and make sure our braw groom scrubs every inch of his body, so he lives up to his famed beauty," she quipped again, laughing at Alex's scowl. He moved towards the door, but then stopped and took an overzealous bow.

"But alas, my beauty is but a curse, my dear Izzy. See the hand fate has dealt me? Marriage." His tone became increasingly dramatic to match his performance.

Izzy only scoffed; his charm was forever wasted on her, which only encouraged him more as he gave her a wink.

"Ye ken ye missed yer calling as a mummer, Alex; though I wouldnae pay a coin to see ye." The slightly bemused, slightly disgusted expression was back on Izzy's face. "Ye are twenty-six years going on seventeen years. Time to grow up, laddie."

"Come, man. My wife has spoken and ye ken I do as she says, and so will ye," smiled Jamie to Izzy, as he and Alex left the room. "Dinnae fash, I will have him back shortly, *leannan.*"

Jamie and Alex headed to the loch within the perimeter of Alex's keep, Castle Balla Cloiche. Simply translated, it meant 'wall of stone'. The MacNichol lands were curtained by a wall of stone that extended well past the keep and onto their demesne lands. In the last few years, due to Alex's socialising and his father's erratic behaviour, the town was generally busy with passersby and the local tavern was renowned for its rowdy behaviour.

Alex thought of his own behaviour. He was aware he had been churlish, but he and Jamie had been friends for too long to let that impact their bond. Clamping his hand on Jamie's shoulder, he expelled a long breath, coming to terms with what the day before him held.

"Och, Jamie, my old friend, tell me – what have ye heard?"

Jamie let out a grin. He knew Alex was slowly coming to accept what would soon take place.

"I ken yer keen to hear aboot her looks, but I have nae heard much. But, I have heard other information aboot yer soon-to-be bride."

Jamie paused, purposely wanting Alex to have to ask for more information. Alex gave him a sideways glance, opened his mouth, but clamped it shut again. He heard a snicker from Jamie and ignored it. To annoy him further, Jamie started to whistle a happy tune. Alex, now grinding his teeth, held back a rude retort. *'Tis what he wants*, he thought, his ire already cooling. Having no brother himself, Alex loved the camaraderie he'd had with Jamie since they were little lads, and knew the traps Jamie would lay to get a rise out of him.

They reached the loch and began to strip. Jamie threw a bar of scented soap at Alex, who caught it in one hand. As he stepped into the icy water, he took a deep inhale and smelt sandalwood and rosemary – a typical earthy but indulgent soap, made by Izzy.

"Give yerself a good scrub. If I ken my bonnie wife, she will give ye a good whiff to make sure ye cleaned yerself up right."

Alex rolled his eyes in response, but the grin on his face belied his annoyance. Izzy was an extraordinary woman. Her courtship with Jamie had been turbulent and passionate. Despite her bonnie looks, after seeing the love the two shared and coming to care for her as a sister, Alex could never imagine Izzy in his bed. Not that he would ever admit that to Jamie, since every now and then it was fun to ignite his jealousy.

"What are ye grinning aboot?" called Jamie. "Ye look a wee bit wicked."

"None of yer business," Alex countered, as he soaped his braw chest into a lather, the suds glistening off his tanned skin. Thinking back to what Jamie knew, he became more and more curious. Ducking his body in the water to rinse off, he swore an oath in his head. Rising up, he pegged the soap at Jamie.

"Alright, ye gobshite, tell me what ye ken and quit yer smirking!"

Chuckling, Jamie exited the loch and started to dry off. "It is nothing of great import; more interesting. Yer lassie was engaged before ye, to an Englishman named Gilbert Percy, a baron. Some childhood friend of hers. The lad died in a border skirmish. One of the Bruce's men told me he was kenned to have a black heart – nae the kind of man ye want yer daughter to marry."

Alex pondered the information. *What are the chances she is still untouched?* He shook his head. *Like that is going to matter.* For the first time in his life, he found himself reluctant to bed a woman.

"Thank ye, Jamie. Now, if I have any disgruntled Englishmen show up on my doorstep, I will ken it's this dead fiancé's family wanting back what's theirs."

"Possibly. But, dinnae ye forget, the Bruce negotiated this wedding as an alliance to keep some peace between the Border Scots and the English."

"Well, why did he nae arrange that with a Border Scot,

or handfasting?" Alex asked without guile, knowing that the Bruce would have confided the inner workings of his mind to Jamie. They had all been friends and allies for many years and he knew how Jamie and the Bruce enjoyed nothing more than discussing strategy.

"Och, Alex, ye ken handfasting takes a year and a day. That willnae suit his purposes. The alliance works as ye are Scot and she is English, but up here in the Highlands with ye, she will be far enough from her family if her intent is to stir trouble. And the English are nae that fond of coming deep into our Highlands."

What Jamie said rang true – the Bruce was known for his good sense of strategy. *I should have realised there would be no way out*, he thought to himself gloomily. He threw Jamie a glare.

"Ye ken I blame ye, Jamie; ye were the Bruce's first choice."

Jamie gave him a satisfied smile in return. "Aye, but as soon as I spied my Izzy bathing, appearing to me as a water nymph in my fevered state at that time, there was never going to be another woman fer me," Jamie told Alex, with feeling generally uncharacteristic of the skilled warrior.

"Jamie, I tell ye this as my friend: ever since ye fell in love, ye make me sick to be around ye."

Jamie laughed, knowing it was mostly in jest, and he wasn't bothered by the part that wasn't. "Ye ken ye may fall deeply fer this lass. Ye cannae control love. Love is a feeling that takes over yer heart and mind, whether ye want it to or not. Ye can try to resist, my friend, but ye willnae succeed," shared Jamie.

Alex heard his soft words, but sensed no embarrassment. He knew Jamie would always regret the wasted time away from Izzy, due to his own stubbornness.

"And surely, Alex, ye are coming to grow even a little bit tired of yerself and lusty ways, jumping from bed to bed? Ye break all these lassies' hearts, but ye do it so charmingly they still pine fer ye when they should hate ye," Jamie finished with a shake of his head.

Alex did not reply, patting Jamie on the back in acknowledgement, but it played in the back of his mind. He did envy what Jamie shared with Izzy, but he did not think himself capable of such a love. He was too selfish to love someone, compromise, and put their needs before his own. This is why he loved and left them, and always ensured they knew he would offer nothing more than his bed. Not wanting to share these thoughts, especially with his besotted friend and on his own undesired wedding day, he forced one of his charming grins onto his face. *'Tis ill-fated as it is*, he thought, *but I am a man without a choice, except to make what I can of this farce.* Throwing his arm around his best friend's shoulder, he stared up at his stone keep, bustling with people preparing for a wedding.

"Put the shackles on me, Jamie. I am ready to meet my fate that is marriage."

Chapter Two

Lady Grace Worthington rode along in the enclosed wooden cart with her maid, Nanny Bea. It jostled as they hit an uneven patch in the road, which had them uncomfortably bumping and sliding around on the seat. This was the first time in her eighteen years that she had left the lands of her home. It was a shame her father had not wanted to send her off in one of the better carriages, but seeing as she would not return, Grace could see why. Her father's own men weren't even escorting her into the cold, blustery Highlands; the King of Scotland's guards had taken on the task instead.

Shifting again in her seat and finding no comfort, she looked heavenward for resilience. Instead, she was greeted by a sharp gust of wind that entered through the uneven slats and seemed to cut straight through her thick woollen stockings. Bouncing around on the thinly-cushioned wooden seats had her feeling as if a horse had kicked her in the derriere, with a firm hoof on each cheek. Looking at Nanny, she swallowed her guilt. *If 'tis uncomfortable for me, what of poor Nanny?* Nanny, though a true saint, was already a woman when Grace was born and now at Grace's eighteen years, considerably older and grey. She never complained through the long days of this arduous journey, but Grace knew her aged bones probably ached.

Grace's sickly mother passed when she was very young. She had little memory of her, even before her passing. Her father, Lord Alfric Worthington, indulged her when she was young but had grown distant as she grew older. His moods were sometimes dark and unpredictable. She taught herself how to be inconspicuous in his presence, only truly coming alive in his absence. She never learned why he was this way, but remembered Nanny whispering to her once when she was little that some people are just born mean.

Thinking of what she was leaving behind caused her to shiver. She was free, but for how long? What if this Scotsman was a hulking, uncouth brute? From what she had heard, the English always described Scots as such. She pulled her beige shawl tighter around her body as her nerves did funny things to her insides, as they always did when she felt any angst.

"Are you alright, my dear child?" asked Nanny, her aged brow wrinkled in concern.

"I am, Nanny; I am just wool-gathering," Grace said, forcing a smile.

"Come now, you know you cannot hide things from me."

"I was just thinking of our journey and what awaits us. The men escorting us said we would arrive today, so I am starting to feel nervous."

Nanny nodded in sympathy. She was the only one who

knew of her nervous spells. "'Tis a fresh start for you, lovey. I have a good feeling about what awaits."

"You are ever the optimist, Nanny, and I do love you for it," said Grace, as she reached over and squeezed her hand in a comforting gesture. "How are you faring, Nanny? I imagine you must be sore?"

She surprised Grace with a chuckle. "Do not worry for me, child. Nanny's posterior has enough padding to keep me comfortable," she smiled, pointing to her buttocks. Grace could not help but laugh, appreciating the mood lightening.

The wheels ticked over and over, the dull thud and click becoming a steady rhythm in her mind. Time seemed to speed up as she heard one of the men yell out that they would soon arrive at Castle Balla Cloiche. Her new home. *I wonder what the words mean. Surely this new home cannot be any worse than my old one, or the one I almost ended up at.* As always, when she thought of her dead fiancé, an icy hand squeezed her heart. To be fair, she had always known him, but never got to truly know him. All she learned were whispers from others of his dark nature, and the way his gaze made her panic. *Be positive, Grace, and think happy thoughts.*

As the cart bolted up the path to Castle Balla Cloiche, she opened the curtain to watch the scene before her unfold. The first thing she noted was the people, staring and pointing. Giving a tentative wave and smile, she received blank stares in return. With a sigh, she turned her gaze up ahead and saw a magnificent castle. The tall stone ramparts were an impressive sight and the fine and sturdy workmanship of the structure belied its age. When she compared the manor house she lived in to this magnificent structure, she thought it more impressive than her own home.

As they drew through the gate into the courtyard, she saw a group of people standing and waiting. Two extremely large men and two small women stood slightly in front, and she could sense a mix of tension and excitement. They had not noticed her peeking out the window and when the cart stopped, Nanny exited first, ready to help Grace climb out. She still had an eye on the quartet and saw the dark-haired man, who was quite handsome, grimace when he looked at Nanny; the fair-haired man, also attractive, stood beside him and elbowed him in the ribs. Frowning to herself, Grace wondered what he was so displeased about. *Maybe no one told him about Nanny. Great, I have annoyed the man before we have even met. Too bad for him, Nanny is my non-negotiable!*

Nanny poked her head back in the cart. "Are you coming out, child?" she asked with an outstretched hand.

Grace inhaled deeply. Taking Nanny's hand, she exited the cart, feeling the rush of blood flowing to her legs as she stood on her feet. Steadying herself, she smoothed down her skirt and looked up. Within a minute, she wished she had never stepped out, the uncomfortable wooden confines suddenly seeming a safe haven. The courtyard was silent, and the awkwardness grew heavier. The courtyard itself was unremarkable. There were some animals walking around; she noticed two goats and a sheep nibbling at hay lying outside of what must be the stable. The dark-haired man stared at her agape, while the other man and women grinned. The woman with the copper hair must have realised they had been standing in silence and she suddenly clapped her hands.

"Welcome to the home of the MacNichols, milady. I am Izzy Murray, and this is my husband, Laird Jamie Murray. This man with his jaw hanging open is yer betrothed,

Alexander MacNichol, and the bonnie lass beside me is his sister, Kenna," she announced, as she elbowed her husband who then elbowed Alexander again. Her betrothed shook his head like he was trying to rid himself of a daze and gave a slight bow.

"Please, call me Alex," he said in an odd voice, like his chest was tight. Grace caught the eye roll Izzy threw at Alex and suppressed the urge to giggle at the random and unexpected gesture.

"Thank you, and I am pleased to meet you all. This is Nanny Bea, my lifelong companion." She emphasised the last two words as she eyed Alex, her heart thumping at her attempt to be bold. Alex just shrugged, turned his back to her, and addressed everyone else standing in the courtyard.

"Right! The Bruce will be here soon, so let us go start merry-making!" he called to the crowd, and sauntered inside as his clansmen cheered.

"*Mo dhia*, he is a *tolla-thon*. Jamie, ye keep him in line and I will see to Grace." Jamie kissed his wife fondly on her cheek and gave a bow to Grace and Nanny before jogging after Alex.

"Please accept my apologies fer that welcome, milady. Yer groom is a wee bit nervous," said Izzy warmly, as she beckoned for Grace and Nanny to follow her. As they entered the Great Hall, Izzy ordered a couple of servants to fetch Grace's belongings, then veered to the right and went up a spiral staircase.

Grace gave Izzy and Kenna warm smiles and said, "Please, call me Grace." *Izzy is so self-assured. I envy her this*, Grace sighed inwardly. Kenna, while appearing friendly, seemed a little shy.

"Thank ye, Grace. Ye, Kenna, and myself will be fine friends – just ye wait and see. And ye too, Nanny," said Izzy, patting the older woman's elbow.

Nanny, surprised but happy with the familiar inclusion, whispered to Grace, "I have a very good feeling about this, my child."

They reached a room just as servants were coming out, and stopped at the door. Izzy entered first, her eyes appraising the room and her pert nose sniffing the air.

"Ahhh, that will do nicely," she said, satisfied.

"Ye always manage miracles, Izzy," said Kenna, sniffing a vase of wildflowers.

Grace took in the room. It was clean, with minimal but well-crafted furniture. But, it was clear this was a guest room, and not a room adjoining the Laird's. Izzy had been watching the expression on Grace's face.

"I am verra bossy, Grace, but I thought ye and Alex may want to decide whether or nae to share a bedroom. Nae that he will mind, ye ken, but I wanted ye to have some space before moving in," Izzy explained.

Grace and Kenna both blushed at the unspoken suggestion of Alex and Grace sharing a bed.

"Thank you, Izzy. I was expecting my own room, but I thought it would be joined to the Laird's; but I guess Alex's father has that room?"

Kenna shook her head. "Nay, Alex does have the Laird's room, which is grand. His room is above this one we are standing in, and mine is two rooms down from yers," Kenna explained.

"Why did ye think ye and Alex would have separate rooms at all?" asked Izzy curiously.

"That is how my parents were," Grace said, now feeling awkward. "I did not think a man and woman shared. Do you and your husband share? What of privacy?" Grace was now the curious one.

"Aye, Jamie and I share. I cannae imagine nae waking up beside him now. And fer privacy, we have the women's solar where we ladies go to spend time. Jamie and his brothers may stop in, but we are usually embroidering or stitching, so they have little interest," Izzy said with an eyeroll, and Kenna giggled. It was clear to Grace that the two were close, and she felt a pang of envy at never having a friend close in age of her own.

"He is a handsome devil," said Nanny. "I see beautiful babies to take care of – I have a good feeling about this wedding." She repeated her earlier sentiments as she shuffled around the room.

Nanny's positive outlook, whilst in goodwill, just made Grace more nervous. And he was a very handsome man – maybe too handsome. The troubled thought must have shown on her face, as she felt a comforting pat on the shoulder.

"Dinnae fash, Grace, ye do what feels right fer now. Marriage is an adjustment, and if Alex gives ye any trouble, ye tell me or Kenna, ye ken?" Izzy stated firmly.

"Aye, Grace, please do. Alex hates when we are displeased with him and he will surely become that way with ye. And I am verra excited to have another woman around here!" Kenna added, her initial shyness now ebbing. Grace felt a warm glow in her chest. It was the feeling of acceptance, and something new – camaraderie. She had few friends her own age, and she felt a little giddy. She was almost giddier at the prospect of friendship than that of her wedding.

"What does Balla Cloiche mean?" she asked, remembering her earlier curiosity. Kenna laughed before answering, and apologised when she saw the confused look on Grace's face.

"Och, sorry, Grace; it is nae ye I laugh at, but translating it will sound so uninteresting. It means 'wall of stone'."

"I much prefer the Gaelic way, I think," Grace giggled. "On that, I will need to learn more Gaelic in general. I heard so much of it spoken today."

"Aye, but Izzy and I will teach ye," Kenna warmly assured her.

Izzy called for a bath and soon a steaming tub was before Grace, and a screen placed for privacy. She removed her hair covering and shook out the soft golden tresses. Settling her sore, aching body into the lavender-scented water, she sighed with relief. The warmth removed the last of the cold that had settled in her bones, and for a moment she felt only pure pleasure.

As Grace washed behind the wooden divider and chatted with the women on the other side, she truly felt she could learn to be happy here. Izzy and Kenna had taken to Nanny Bea instantly and were talking about healing herbs, a topic Izzy and Kenna seemed very passionate about. To spend her days filled with purpose, *enjoyable* purpose, with likeminded people was a dream come true for Grace.

A knock at the door broke her reverie, and she wondered how long she had been soaking for as she examined the pruned skin of her fingers. A muffled male voice called through the door and spoke to Izzy.

"The Bruce is here, *mo chridhe*, and the clan assembled. Will ye be ready soon?" asked Jamie.

Grace, now in a panic, jumped up from the bath with a

splash, grabbed the drying cloth, and peeked out at the women from behind the divider.

"Aye, we will be down shortly!" Izzy yelled back to her husband, giving Grace a comforting wink.

"Aye, *mo chridhe*," Jamie replied, and they heard him walk away.

Kenna looked at Grace and explained, "*Mo chridhe* means 'my heart'."

"Oh, that is beautiful," Grace replied wistfully. How wonderful for Izzy to be loved so unabashedly.

"Grace, yer a natural beauty and need no primping. Let us dress ye and brush out yer hair, and we will be done," said Izzy as she shook out Grace's clothing.

"Can I wear it out before I am married?" she asked, unsure of Scottish customs.

Izzy shrugged, unconcerned. "I am nae the best guide fer that, but I never cover my hair, nor does Kenna. Our clans do nae stand on ceremony. Ye will come to see that we are simple people, Grace," Izzy assured her warmly, "and ye have such a beautiful shade of hair."

Unaccustomed to such compliments, Grace blushed. What did tradition matter, so far away from all she knew, deep in these foreign lands? Izzy seemed so eager, and Grace was happy to appease her. And Alex may feel the same way about her hair, and she wanted to please him also. She took a deep breath. "I am in your hands, Izzy."

Chapter Three

The Great Hall, at Izzy's instruction, was brimming with scattered wildflowers and the reeds carpeting the floor had been refreshed. Alex, however, was oblivious to the changes. He stood with the Bruce and Jamie, but paid no attention. In comparison to the morn, he was now completely sober. Between the icy bath in the loch and the sight of his bride's beauty, which had slapped him in the face when she stepped out of the cart, it felt like days since he'd had a drop of ale. *Aye, still English, but nae the pale nag I envisioned,* he thought incredulously. His right-hand man, Aran, had been as agape as he, also convinced that Alex was going to get the raw end of this arrangement.

Grace, his soon-to-be bonnie bride, equaled Izzy's famed beauty, if not surpassed it. Her skin was fair, but rather than pale, was more hued to the glow of the late summer sunset. Her hair, from what he could tell from the tucked up plaited tresses peeking out from under her head-dress, was like spun golden silk – thick and shiny. The head-dress itself was plain and unadorned, which only enhanced the fact she needed no aid with her beauty.

"Alex! Alex! Are ye with us, or does my dear wife need to throw another pitcher in yer face?" asked Jamie, as the Bruce laughed. Scowling, Alex brushed them both off, annoyed they had interrupted his musings.

"What do ye want my attention fer, Jamie?"

"The lassies will be down soon. I dinnae think ye heard me before. Too distracted by yer bonnie bride?" Jamie replied with a wink.

Now guffawing, the Bruce joined in. "Alex, I must say I am offended ye thought I would wed ye to a 'nag', as ye so put it to Jamie. The most braw man in Scotland needs a beauty to match his own. Though, I dinnae think any lass will be pleased with the broken hearts ye have strewn across Scotland."

Jamie gave the Bruce a sideways smile. "Dinnae ye ken, Alex gives them a stern word beforehand. He says, 'I will love ye and leave ye, lass. That is all I can offer ye.' If it wasn't fer his face, he would still be an untried lad with that shite."

Alex rolled his eyes at them both. "Oh, the wit of ye both. Wonderful mummers ye would make," he muttered, causing his man Aran's eyebrows to raise and look to the Bruce. But there was no concern to be had, as the Bruce slapped Alex on the back with a great bellow of laughter. "But, I admit my bride is bonnie; perhaps even more than Izzy, Jamie," Alex said slyly.

"Nay! No one can match my bonnie lass!" Jamie protested, before his fierce expression dropped back into laughter. "I will never forget when her Nanny stepped out and ye thought she was to be yer bride!" This sent Jamie and the Bruce into another fit of laughter.

Alex rolled his eyes again, but before he could respond, he heard the commotion of the ladies arriving. Then he heard the 'oohs' and 'aahs' of the clan as they laid eyes upon his bride. Her hair was now uncovered, the spun golden strands now lush waves, forming an angelic halo over her goddess face. Aye, she was Aphrodite rising from the foam; full heart-shaped lips, high cheekbones, and deep blue eyes that shone like sapphires. And what made her even more beautiful, was how completely unaware she was of the perfect picture she made.

Grace had since stifled her jittery nerves, so was no longer trembling. She now only felt a numbness pulsating through her limbs. She quickly scanned the Great Hall, and a sea of eyes and faces passed in a blur. She looked down at her satin-covered feet and took a deep breath before raising her eyes again, this time directing them towards the front. She saw the King of Scotland, her husband-to-be, and his stalwart friend Laird Murray, their expressions at this distance scrutinising and hawkish.

"Come on, lovey. Move your feet," whispered Nanny.

Planting a frozen smile on her face, she started to walk towards the men, but focused her eyes on Alex. The closer she got, she realised the mistake in this, as he truly was the most handsome man she had ever seen, and foreign feelings began to flutter in her stomach. It was a combination of nerves and excitement, but now that she could see his eyes, trepidation set in. There was no expression in his eyes; the deep blue was endless, but emotionless.

The Bruce's booming voice broke her reverie, causing

her to jump a little, and she caught the little upturn of Alex's lip as he noticed. Annoyed at his amusement, she stood by his side and faced the Bruce ahead of him, refusing to let show that her nerves had been triggered. Despite his aloofness, something in his presence gave her a sense of security. Was it his bulk? Or her intuition trying to give her a hint? It irked her even more that he allowed her to feel safe, annoyed, and anxious all at once, as a butterfly seemingly caught in her heart and its wings rapidly beat against her chest.

"'Tis I, yer King, who will bless this marriage today. I made arrangements fer the banns to be read throughout the Highlands. A union between Scotland and England. A testament to us all, that we can live in harmony. I bless the union between Alexander MacNichol and Lady Grace Worthington on this day at Castle Balla Cloiche. Ye both may now seal this blessed union with a kiss."

Grace saw Alex's face coming towards her and she watched open-eyed as he placed a chaste kiss on her parted lips. The feeling of physical contact, *intimate* contact at that, shook her to the very depths of her core as she tried to comprehend the reactions of her body.

Whatever words came next did not resonate in her mind as she worked on steadying her racing heart. *Drats, I was doing so well!* Only Nanny knew her secret – 'the breath attacks', they called them. When her heart beat so fast, it thundered in her ears like the worst of storms. The difficulty to draw a full and even breath. Sweat beading on her body as the perspiration broke free from her skin. She had worked so well at keeping herself calm and her breath attacks had grown more infrequent, but she was idiotic to believe she would make it through this day on a cloud of calm.

"Grace, Grace, are ye alright?" Izzy's voice broke its way through her panicked state, and she focused on calming her breath.

She looked around, hoping no one else had noticed, and thankfully saw Izzy standing by her side while Alex's large body had mainly shielded her from the clan. While there was laughter and chatter all around her, she could not ascertain if anyone else had seen. She saw Alex eyeing her shrewdly, yet with a hint of compassion.

"Are ye alright, Grace?" Izzy asked again urgently, her concern apparent.

"Yes, yes, I am fine. I just need some air," Grace said, forcing a smile in the hope to convince them everything was fine. She knew Scots could be superstitious at best, and she did not want to make such a poor impression on her first day.

"Of course, dinnae fash. Let us take a walk outside," Izzy said, as she linked arms with Grace. "What say ye, Alex?" she then asked pointedly, noting Alex had been staring at them.

"I ... uh ... aye, Izzy, thank ye. Take Grace fer a walk and get her some air," said Alex quietly, flustered at being put on the spot. His handsome face failed to hide a slight flush.

Nanny had since melted into the crowd, so Grace clung to Izzy's arm as her only support. She saw Izzy throw a long-suffering look at Alex. "Let us go, Grace. It appears chivalry is missing in this present company."

Alex was puzzled. What caused the sudden change from her cool demeanour to a breathless and wide-eyed panic?

He could not help but feel guilty, since what else but the Bruce blessing their wedding, and his own kiss on her lips, could cause such a reaction? She was clearly as innocent as they came, for a kiss so chaste to affect her so. The raw vulnerability drew at his heartstrings, and he wanted to pull her into his arms, but his body had turned wooden. For the first time in his life, a woman had taken his sense of control.

"What has ye lookin' like ye have seen a ghost, Alex?" asked Jamie with concern.

One of the men overheard and crudely quipped, "Aye, it's the ghosts of his former bedmates waving goodbye to him!"

A ruckus of laughter erupted and Alex forced a smile and laughed along. He accepted a flagon of ale and two cups from a serving lass and pulled Jamie away, the jesting men entertaining the Bruce.

Finding a quieter spot, Alex poured the two of them a drink. "I will warn ye that yer bonnie wife is nae too happy with me," Alex began, knowing Izzy would rage at them both later.

"Is that what gave ye a fright?" asked Jamie with a smile. "Dinnae fash. Since when *is* she happy with ye?" he said, finishing with a laugh.

Alex gave him a wry smile. "Aye, 'tis true, but this time it was something entirely different. I dinnae ken what exactly, but I have an idea."

Jamie waited for him to continue.

"Grace appeared to have a reaction of some sort. As if she was reacting poorly to our marriage, to my kiss; I am nae sure. What I am sure of is that I handled the whole situation poorly."

"'Twas most likely nerves, Alex. Ye cannae blame yerself. And I will speak with Izzy if ye like?"

Alex grinned at his friend, a revered laird and warrior, posing this offer with an air of trepidation.

"Nay, dinnae fash, I willnae make ye take on my wee wife!" Jamie told him, laughing.

"Her ire was more directed at me nae helping to provide some comfort to Grace, I think. Izzy, of course, is taking care of it fer me," Alex acknowledged, feeling sheepish.

Jamie put his arm around his shoulder and gave him a shake. "Come on, let us get some food to soak up the ale, so ye make no more mistakes and don't piss off my wife fer the rest of the day."

Alex thought maybe he was just being silly, and it was only a bout of nerves. Being wed to a stranger would bring out nerves from many women. But, he had a niggling feeling it was more than that, and he made a mental note to think more upon it when he was alone.

Grace was so very grateful for Izzy and this instant camaraderie that had blossomed between them. Their turn in the crisp Scottish air, and Izzy not asking questions, helped her recover quickly. Still feeling slightly embarrassed that her new husband had also seen what had transpired, she prepared herself to pass it off as a dizzy spell if he asked. Young ladies were known to be light of heart, were they not? Though, it did not seem likely he would ask.

Once back in the Great Hall, she was seated at the main table between Alex, who had not even spared her a glance, and the King of Scotland, holding court in his booming voice. She held back a sigh and focused on the food in front of her. The various meat and fish dishes turned her stomach slightly, so Grace placed some oat bread drizzled with honey and a pear on her plate. Izzy's spot was a few seats down, so they could not talk together. Picking at the food would have to keep her occupied while she sat here like an outlander.

The walk with Izzy in the fresh air had helped clear her mind a little, and something had occurred to her. She pressed two fingers to her mouth as she realised the feel of Alex's lips pressed against her own had actually left her feeling comforted, not afraid. She entertained the idea that signals from her body did not always have to mean danger.

When she and Izzy had returned to the Great Hall, the wedding ceremony seemed a distant memory as the clan celebrated the free-flowing *uisge beatha* and the copious amounts of food. The ceremony was a transaction; the celebrations were what all the people really looked forward to. As the day settled to night, Izzy had warned her that the clan would become raucous and to not be alarmed – a Highland wedding, like any other Scottish celebration, was not a sedate affair.

"How did ye find yer wedding day, milady?" asked the Bruce kindly as he turned towards her, interrupting her thoughts. Perhaps he had heard her thoughts and took pity on her. In his stately crown and thick fur-lined coat of his kinghood, he appeared intimidating, but his pleasant manner shone through. Usually, being close to a dominant male in power – someone like her father – would be daunting to Grace. But, the Bruce, with his warm smile and twinkling brown eyes, put her at ease.

"It was lovely, Your Grace. I am indebted to Lady Murray for all her assistance today," she replied graciously.

"Aye, our Izzy has a firm hand," he said with a grin, "and I hoped ye two would hit it off. I ken it must be hard fer ye, coming to a new land – different customs and all." He gestured to their surroundings.

Grace nodded, taking a sip of the spiced mulled wine before looking around the Great Hall at the sea of merry-making faces. "It is hard. But, I did not find myself overly attached to my home, with the exception of my Nanny Bea, who has journeyed with me to stay." She blushed at the Bruce's raised eyebrows at her forthright comment about home.

"I am glad to hear it. If ye ever need anything, ye have Alex of course, but ye can always send word to me or the Murrays, ye ken?"

She managed a nod, as emotion caught in her throat. This stranger held more warmth in his welcome than her own father had in his goodbye. Grace sensed eyes studying her from the side where Alex sat, and she slowly turned around, taking another fortifying sip of wine. Her own blue eyes clashed with his. She watched as his pupils dilated under the intense gaze that trapped them both, and wondered what her own eyes were doing.

"Are ye feeling better, lass?" he asked, in a low and gentle tone. The warm timbre washed over her like she had just sat in front of a fire.

"Yes, I am, thank you. 'Twas just a dizzy spell," she said, giving him a weak smile.

He said nothing, and Grace could tell her response left him unconvinced. She broke the intensity of their gaze and looked down at his hands. She watched as his finger circled the rim of his cup. His hands were large and tanned, rough but comforting at the same time.

Eventually, Alex spoke. "If ye need anything, be sure to ask me or Kenna. I will acquaint yer Nanny Bea with my household on the morrow and ensure they ken anything she requests is at her disposal also."

"I appreciate that. When should I meet the household and discuss the management of the keep?" she asked, since this was something she was trained to do.

"Yer services will nae be needed. I am nae yer Laird, and I dinnae see any reason to change up the household."

His response was not said cruelly, but still held a firmness that made her feel a need to apologise as if she had said something wrong. Holding back the urge, she was about to ask instead how he would like her to spend her days, when she felt a hand on her shoulder. Turning around she saw Izzy, Kenna, and Nanny Bea behind her.

"We have come to get ye prepared fer yer wedding night, if yer ready?" Something in Izzy's tone told her that if she said no, she would assist in barring Alex from her bed without any further explanation. Laughing out loud at the thought, she nodded at the quizzical faces of the women before her. Gulping down the rest of her wine in one mouthful, she stood up. Without sparing Alex another glance, lest it weakened her resolve, she said, "Let us go."

Chapter Four

Alex's bedchamber was large, which was fortunate seeing as the bed seemed so large it took up an unordinary amount of space. *Then again my husband to me was also very large*, thought Grace as she pictured his muscular build. Grace sensed Izzy had ordered the room freshly cleaned, as the fresh scent of wildflowers permeated the air. A washstand, chamber pot, and divider stood in the corner, and Izzy called her over.

"Ye can freshen up over here and there is a chamber pot fer yer needs. Where we came up the stairs, if ye keep walking down, ye will find the family garderobes as well. When ye need a bath, the servants will bring one up. But, dinnae fash, Kenna is working on a bathing room to be set up, just like I have back home."

Izzy continued to chatter on as Nanny Bea brushed Grace's hair and Kenna searched through her belongings for a night-shift. Looking from the chamber pot to the bed, it began to dawn on her that she would now be sharing her personal space with a man. She knew there would surely be moments of privacy, but everything else would need to be a huge adjustment, and she felt her nerves stir.

Grace was lost in her thoughts, and it took Izzy a few moments of saying her name before she caught her attention. "Sorry, Izzy, my mind oft floats away with the faeries."

"Dinnae fash. I wanted to ask if ye had any questions aboot tonight?" Izzy, normally so self-assured, blushed at the intimate topic she was not accustomed to discussing with others.

Grace took a moment before she responded. Did she know what took place on a wedding night? Yes. The man takes the woman and they become one. It will hurt. It will not last long. It is a woman's duty, and soon she shall bear the fruit of their union. Nanny had explained this to her. She assumed there was more to it, but as with any topic that made her uncomfortable, she avoided talking or thinking about it. However, after meeting Alex and experiencing the strange effect he had on her body, she was curious. The effects were not unpleasant; if anything, they stirred new pleasant feelings. But, she did not know how to explain them, so kept quiet and went with a conservative response.

"I understand the general expectation. Can I ask you, though – as a married woman, how would you explain it?" Grace was unable to mask the curiosity in her voice. Izzy signalled for Kenna and Nanny Bea to move away, and they quickly hurried to the other end of the room to busy themselves.

"'Tis something that will be different fer everyone. Fer me, from the verra first time I laid my eyes upon Jamie, I wanted him in a way I had never felt before. And then, his first touch, the first kiss ... och, it was like nothing I had ever felt. I still get the same feeling; he just has to look at me a certain way. There is nothing to feel ashamed or embarrassed aboot. Being naked with one another is such an uninhibited feeling, so primal."

Nanny and Kenna had been busy lighting candles. Grace was able to watch the dreamy gaze fall over Izzy's face and felt a pang of envy. She wanted to feel this way, to feel this joy.

Izzy noticed Grace staring, waiting for her to continue, and her cheeks pinkened slightly. "Sorry, Grace, I drifted off! Tonight is aboot *ye*, and wonderful feelings aside, 'tis important ye ken that the first time, ye may feel some discomfort. But, Alex ... well, let us just say that Alex is, uh, *skilled* in these areas." Izzy was clearly at a loss at how to explain that Grace's new husband was more skilled in this area than she; but anyone would be, especially with Grace being a virgin.

"Thank you, Izzy, I appreciate it. I wish there was time to get to know him before doing something so ... so ... intimate?" Grace did not know how to explain that except for Nanny, she had little comfort or affection in her life.

And to be naked? How do I give and receive such affections like this to a stranger?

A sharp tap on the door put a stop to their conversation and they watched as Kenna opened it and hailed Izzy over. Izzy gave Grace a quick hug and wished her well, and told her to send word if she needed anything. Nanny Bea guided Grace to the bed and as she settled, she heard Izzy let out an expletive as she left the room, causing Grace to jump and her nerves to spike. Nanny patted her hand as they waited and reassured her all would be well. There was another tap at the door, and Nanny gave her a kiss on the forehead and walked over to open the door. As she watched Nanny exit, she saw the large outline of her husband enter.

His chiselled face was accentuated by the glow of

candlelight, and she watched his face as he searched her own.

"Good eve, wife," he said in a stiff voice.

"Good eve, husband," she countered, as she pulled the covers up a little higher.

She observed him as he went over to the wash stand to freshen up, splashing water on his face, his back to her. He was still for a moment, but then started to remove his surcoat and boots. He pulled his leine up and over his head, exposing his torso and broad shoulders, the muscles tanned and defined, but he did not remove his braies. He turned around to face her.

"Do ye ken what happens between a man and a woman on their wedding night?" he asked, as he walked slowly to the bed.

Watching him for the last few minutes had stirred a yearning within her and her mouth had become dry, so all she could do was nod. Alex sighed.

"I see ye are nervous, lass; dinnae fash. I willnae make ye do anything ye dinnae want to do," he said in a now gentle voice. He lifted the cover to slide into bed beside her. His body heat settled on her like the warmth of a sunny day, and she felt her body lose some tension. He left space between them and turned on his side to look at her. He eyed her face intently and she started to stress, that anxious feeling stirring, worried he was finding fault. They sat in silence for a moment, the only sounds in the room their breath, oddly but nicely in unison. The in-tune rhythm made her feel at ease.

"Ye are nae what I expected. Ye are verra beautiful." His tone held a hint of awe as his voice broke the silence.

"What were you expecting?" Her fears now abated,

Grace was a little confused by his statement. "A hideous bride?"

"Aye, I was, if ye want me to be honest. I have seen Englishwomen, and they left much to be desired."

Alex's blunt response made her laugh involuntarily, the horror in his voice genuine but absurd, and he shook his head in surprise.

"I must confess, I had heard the same about the Scots, especially the ones who live deep in the Highlands. You were not what I was expecting, either."

He waited on the pause, waiting for a compliment in return, but he must have seen the humour in her eyes as she kept her comments to herself. "'Tis good to see ye have a sense of humour as well," he said in a wry tone, as he swept his eyes over her again, scorching her with heat.

The scrutiny of his gaze left her torn. She found herself in new territory, wanting the touch of another, of a man, but she could not help but feel cautious.

"Are you sure it would be alright if we waited, at least for the night?" Grace said quietly, feeling safe to ask, since he had offered.

Alex nodded. "Of course. I dinnae say things unless I mean them. Ye will come to learn this aboot me, amongst other things, as I will ye."

Despite it not even having been a full day since she had met him, she intrinsically knew in that moment she could trust him, and that feeling gave her such a sense of relief that the exhaustion of the journey caught up with her. Her nervous system, no longer in a state of fight or flight, was ready to rest. Bringing one hand to her mouth as a yawn escaped, she reached out with the other and squeezed his much larger hand with her own.

"Thank you, husband. I wish you sweet dreams."

Turning over to face away from him, Grace closed her eyes and allowed herself to drift into a surprisingly peaceful slumber.

Alex would deny this to anyone who asked, but he found himself entranced with his new bonnie bride. She was beautiful and pleasant. *English, and still much to learn of her, aye; but it could have been worse.* His lower half was protesting, his natural carnal urges responding to the situation as they normally would. But, as much as he would love to ravish her, he wanted her to want it, too.

He had not forgotten her earlier reaction, and lying in bed with her now he could feel the tension ebb and flow within her body. The moment she relaxed she was susceptible, and while he may be a philanderer who did not intend to settle down, he was not a heartless bastard. She shared his name, home, and bed now, and he would protect her. His instincts bellowed to him that something about her truly needed protecting, and he wanted to make her feel safe. He would make her safe.

That aside, he did not see why his everyday life would need to change too much. *There will be only little changes, like I will ken who will be waiting for me in bed every night.* He gave her soft profile a side glance and held back a sigh. A sigh of disappointment or contentment he asked himself inwardly? Not wanting to ponder the answer, he moved his thoughts to his duties. Lying on his back and staring up at the ceiling, he listened to her light, even breaths and mulled the day over and thought of the upcoming days, but his mind could not help but drift back to navigating life with his new bride.

And of course, Da would soon be home, causing the usual chaos. Och, I need to get some sleep before I can sort out my thoughts.

In his slumber, Alex felt Grace stir and roll over closer. Her face was now turned towards him, the tip of her nose almost touching his shoulder, and he felt her light breath blow against his skin. *Do I pull her in my arms? Nay!* Not one to endorse cuddling, less it resulted in unrealistic expectations, he pondered this new-found urge for intimacy. He could fall back asleep and ignore her closeness, but the urge to pull her close was stronger. Slightly disgusted with himself for feeling so ... well ... so *Jamie-like* when it came to Izzy, he closed his eyes, but within a few moments, they shot open again in resignation. He lifted his arm so it rested behind her head and gently pulled her closer, so her face now rested on his chest, under his arm. She moved and for a moment he worried he had erred, but he felt her arm cross his chest and curl up as she moved in closer. Pleased with her reaction, he closed his eyes again.

Grace was having the most pleasant dream. She was cocooned in a warm embrace. It was safe and comforting, the feelings foreign, but oh so wonderful. She burrowed deeper, snuggling her face, wanting more of this feeling. As her mind seeped more into consciousness she noted the feeling of skin, smooth and hot, and the tantalising sensation of her own skin pressed against another. She registered the sound of inhalation and slowly opened her eyes in confusion. Her face was resting against a broad chest and the previous day's events came back to her. This was her new husband. And despite the overly intimate position, she felt at ease.

Safe. Something about this man is causing me to feel a peace I have not yet experienced.

She sensed Alex's eyes upon her and boldly she lifted her own to meet his. She did not expect to see the raw, unadulterated fire burning in his blue eyes. She felt her face heat up, but not from embarrassment. She wanted something. Her body was urging her towards something she could not identify; it was all based on physical instinct. Her most feminine part was also heated, and it emboldened her next move. Her palm, resting in the middle of his chest, slid up and she spread her fingers through Alex's lightly sprinkled hair, the sensation of the coarse hair on soft skin under her fingertips sending a shiver up her spine. Grace's eyes still held his and she watched as his pupils dilated and heard his breath become heavy.

Her hand reached his collarbone and she traced the slope of his neck in an upward motion to cup his cheek. Not knowing what to do next, she watched as his lips parted and she moved her thumb to trace his lower lip. Alex gave her a slow sexy grin, the trance he had been ensconced in slightly broken by this gesture, and he gently nipped her thumb before drawing it into his mouth. A rush of heat cascaded over her body. Fascinated by what he was doing, the pounding on the door went unnoticed for a few moments, until she heard Alex mutter what sounded like '*mo dhia*' as he moved out of bed. She heard the door open, and Alex spoke.

"What is it, Kenna?" he asked, his tone exasperated.

"Da's home," Kenna replied, "and I thought ye and Jamie may want to be there when he addresses the Bruce."

"I will be down as soon as I dress. Stay with Grace."

Grace watched him dress hurriedly and exit the room, without even a glance towards her. She heard Kenna walk over and quickly hid her hurt.

"Good morn to ye, Grace," Kenna greeted her cheerily.

"And to you, Kenna. But, pray tell, what is this situation with your father?"

Chapter Five

*H*ow did my morning go from experiencing one of the most erotic moments of my life to running through the keep to deal with the old man?

The thought itself was a blur as Alex rushed to the Great Hall. He saw his father, the Bruce, and Jamie already seated. The Bruce looked amused, Jamie glum, and his dad surly, even more so than normal. At a nearby table were his dad's most faithful men and guard he took everywhere with him.

"Aye, here comes the bonnie groom! My heir – my *only* heir – now married to the bluidy enemy," his dad spat out at him, arms crossed over his chest.

Alex took a seat and poured himself an ale, knowing where this was going. Ewan MacNichol had aged bitterly. Always a man prone to fits of temper, the only person who could manage him was his deceased wife. Gladys MacNichol had passed during Alex's teenage years, while Kenna was just a child, and left an unmanageable husband behind. Ewan liked few things, and disliked many, many things.

He liked hunting, and much of his time was spent away

from the keep. He liked fighting, so when he was home, he spent much of his time in the training fields. He expected all MacNichol men to be strong warriors, and led with a firm hand.

Ewan sorely disliked the English. He thought Robert was soft in trying to make peace and wanted no part of it. But, he was a loyal, proud Scotsman and while he openly disagreed with the Bruce, he would not go against him.

Aye, but the Bruce dinnae have to live with him, Alex thought to himself, as he waited for the tirade to continue.

"Ye can imagine my surprise to come home, after I've been hunting fer food to bring back to my clan – my clan, ye wee gobshite – and see ye have gone and married the English. Ye may as well pierce my heart with ye *sgian dubh* right now, lad." His father's faithful entourage of men all looked at Alex like he was muck underneath their shoes for disappointing his father and Laird by marrying the enemy.

"How can ye be married, lad? Ye have been in and out of more thighs than all the lads in Scotland combined!" Ewan teased him, smiling around at the laughter this caused. "Does yer cold English wife ken ye have never been faithful to one lass? Ye cannae even be faithful to ye father."

Alex still said nothing, knowing interrupting one of his tirades would only prolong it. And he was also glad that the Bruce was taking no insult at the veiled barbs being aimed. Alex took a sip of his ale and watched his father bask in the entertainment he was creating. This meant it was coming to an end.

"I cannae believe yer gonna give me English grandbabies. And seeing as it's ye, I am sure it willnae take long to put it in her belly."

The Bruce cleared his throat, subtly but demanding

authority, and they all turned to face their King. "Enough, Ewan. Let us nae throw stones at babes nae yet born."

Ewan said nothing, realising his grace period was over.

"Da, I am sorry ye were nae consulted. But I, as are ye, am a loyal subject to the Scottish crown. Despite yer dislike fer the English, alliances are needed to keep peace between the Border Scots and English."

Alex ignored the sight of Jamie's eyebrows, raised in amusement at his paraphrasing what Jamie had said to him the day before.

"Ye ken I am nae the marrying kind, so dinnae fash – I kept nothing from ye. Anyway, the lass is quiet, well-bred, and she willnae cause ye any grievances being here."

His father responded with an ill-mannered snort, but again his saying nothing was never a good sign. As soon as their company left, Alex had no doubt he would be in for an earful.

"Come, let us break bread. I am leaving with Jamie today, to escort him and Izzy back to Aberscross, so let us enjoy the last of each other's company." Robert's booming voice, jovial but still authoritative, rang across the Great Hall and the men cheered.

Izzy, Grace, and Nanny Bea were sitting on the bed as Kenna tried to explain her father to them. "Da is ... well, he is just ... he gets frustrated verra quick. He has a short temper." She floundered and looked to Izzy. Izzy knew Kenna was too sweet to say her father hated the English. Izzy, while kind, could be a little more direct and turned to Grace and Nanny Bea.

"Ye ken there are many Scots who still dinnae like the English? Well, Laird MacNichol is one of them. But, dinnae fash; his bark is worse than his bite. His words may be hateful, but trust me, ye will bear him no mind. Ye are stronger than ye think," Izzy said, as she watched Grace's aghast expression.

"I imagine those old hatreds linger. That is what war does," Nanny said wisely, nonplussed by this information. She rubbed Grace's hand, seeing her eyes widen and sensing the panic rising in her.

"So, my new father-in-law and laird of this keep, hates me? Without even meeting me?" Grace questioned her companions in despair, and her breath started to shallow.

"He will change his mind when he gets to see how nice ye are," Kenna said eagerly. "I already ken that after only a short time yesterday."

Izzy eyed Grace curiously and reached into the folds of her kirtle. "Grace, dinnae take any insult, but I noticed ye can get verra nervous. Like now, I can see yer eyes are wide, yer breath has quickened, and there is a slight sheen of sweat on yer face. I have some herbs I took from my medicine bag that may help ye," Izzy said quietly, as she held out her hand to show Grace a purple weed, a brown root, and some green leaves. Intrigued, she moved closer to Izzy to have a closer look. She smelt something sweet and fragrant, and something else with a peculiar odour.

"I am not offended, Izzy. My body, my mind ... I am not sure what it is, but since I was small I have felt myself wanting to flee in panic whenever I feel unsafe, unliked, or within the presence of someone without good intentions." The honest answer popped out of her mouth without a second thought, but she had no regrets as she watched Izzy give a sympathetic nod and felt Kenna move closer and squeeze her shoulder. Her senses were telling her to stay and fight, not run away in fright. Similar to the instantaneous connection with Alex, she knew her new friends would not condemn her.

"What do they do?" she asked Izzy, pointing to the colourful herbs in her hands.

"This here purplish one is lavender, and the green is lemon balm. The one with white petals surrounding the yellow centre here is chamomile. They are verra powerful and calming herbs; ye can brew them as a tea, and add to yer bath or yer soaps. Now, this brown smelly one is called valerian root – 'tis also good to calm, but more at night to help ye sleep if ye need it. Ye have these already planted, as Kenna has been planting her own herb garden fer when ye need, and she can explain their uses in more detail."

Amazed that there were other ways to help her nerves, Grace nodded eagerly.

Izzy pulled one final thing from her kirtle – a small leather drawstring pouch. "Ye can keep them with ye always, in the pockets of yer kirtle like me, or hanging off a belt."

Grace felt tears shimmering in her eyes. Tears of gratitude. "Thank you, thank you so much. This will be a big help to me, Izzy. This is very kind of you."

"Let us brew a quick cup fer ye to drink now before we go downstairs. Be nice fer us all to warm our bones and calm our minds."

Alex, feeling apprehensive, could not help but look up at the stone stairs every few moments. The women would be down shortly, and he hoped Izzy and Kenna had prepared Grace for the Laird MacNichol. So accustomed to his father's tirades, he was fine to shrug them off. He had not expected to be drawn to his bride, but Grace had piqued something inside him – a possessiveness, something primal. *Possibly her sweet innocence, something I am verra much nae accustomed to,* he thought to himself wryly. He knew Grace could not stand up to his dad if the need arose, and that the role would fall to him.

Jamie broke his thoughts as he sat down beside him. In a low voice, he spoke. "Ye look deep in thought, Alex. Something bothering ye? Besides the obvious," asked Jamie, with a sideways glance towards the Laird who was laughing raucously with his men, drinking and eating with minimal decorum.

"I am thinking of Da and Grace living under the same roof. I dinnae ken how I barely thought of it yesterday. Didnae even have a chance to warn her myself aboot his hatred fer the English. Married but a day, and I have let my bonnie bride down," Alex said in a rueful tone.

"I gather that from yer time spent last night, ye have come to care fer the lass? The earlier misgivings ye had are now gone?" Jamie asked curiously.

Realising where Jamie was going with this, Alex clammed up. He did not discuss his feelings, since he never had any to discuss. And he was not about to start at this moment.

"'Tis more that she is my responsibility whether I am happy aboot this marriage or not, ye ken?" he countered, trying to sound disinterested. Jamie's expression remained unconvinced.

"Och, here comes the lass, my new English daughter, come to share my table!" The Laird's voice cut through the chatter of the Great Hall. His statement caused everyone to turn and look at Grace, Izzy, Kenna, and Nanny all walking towards them. Alex saw Izzy give his father a filthy look and poor Kenna looked embarrassed. Grace had a smile frozen on her face. It clenched Alex's heart, as it was the practiced smile of someone who had been in too many situations where a smile was forced.

Luckily for all, the Bruce stood up, welcomed the women to sit down, and made introductions. His intervention allowed only for Ewan to smirk with a short and ungallant bow. The Bruce gestured for Alex, Jamie, and Ewan to follow him, leaving the women to break their fast. Alex hung back, wanting to ensure Grace was alright. After a few moments of silence, as Nanny rubbed Grace's back in sympathy, Izzy cleared her throat, with a slight roll of her eyes towards Alex for not asking the question himself.

"That went better than I thought it would. How do ye feel, Grace?"

Grace pondered her response for a few moments and then a smile, a *genuine* smile, broke across her face. "I feel like I do not care what a grumpy old man has to say."

Izzy grinned at Grace's spirit and Kenna looked relieved.

"Aye, that's the spirit, lass," Alex told her with a clap of his hands. "Now, I better go catch up to them."

Alex and Grace stood side by side in the bailey as they readied to farewell the Murrays. Alex was unsurprised that Grace and Izzy had become friends in such a short period of time. Izzy was warm and insightful. Alex watched Grace from the corner of his eye. There was something about Grace he sensed but had not figured out, but he had a suspicion Izzy had. Alas, there was no time to pull her aside and discuss it, nor did he want to make any admissions to how his new bride had gotten under his skin.

"Ye will have to come to Aberscross soon," Izzy said to Grace, giving Alex a pointed look. "Especially before the babe comes, so I can show ye around before I get too big."

"Of course! I cannot wait. And thank you again for everything you have done for me, Izzy," Grace said, her voice heavy with gratitude.

"Ye will still be the bonniest lass I ever did see, *leanaan*," Jamie told Izzy, as he assisted her in mounting her horse.

Alex rolled his eyes at the overindulgent show of affection. "We will come to visit, as long as Jamie here promises to keep control of his fawning," Alex said, wanting to weigh in. This earned him one last jab in the shoulder before Jamie mounted his own horse.

"Ye just wait, my friend," said Jamie, giving him a wink. "But ye send word if ye need anything, ye ken?"

Ignoring the first comment, Alex gave Jamie his thanks as he and Grace waved them off. As the Murrays rode off, Alex sensed a dark presence and looked up to the battlements to see his father staring down at him and Grace. His expression was too far in the distance to make out, but Alex could feel what the gaze portrayed: pure spite for the bonnie lass beside him. Alex turned to her and caught her gazing up at him, analysing his face. Caught in the act, Grace blushed.

"Forgive me for staring, Alex. It is my first time seeing you properly in the daylight and having an opportunity to really gaze upon you."

Alex scanned her face slowly. The sunlight caused her hair, almost white in its fairness, to shine like a halo. Her blue eyes glittered like a loch in the peak of spring. His gaze caused a blush to pinken across her high cheekbones, and he could not help but grin.

"Aye, 'tis quite different to look at each other in the light of day." She smiled so sweetly, it tugged at something inside him, something foreign, and he immediately broke their stare. "I have to get aboot my day now, lass. Yer Nanny Bea is standing over there. Go to her and then find Kenna to show ye the best places to occupy yerself."

Feeling a twinge of guilt at her confused and hurt expression, he quickly turned his back and walked away.

I cannae allow this lass to be my Achilles heel.

Grace watched her husband walk away, tall and confident, and she had the urge to run after him and kick him in one of his shapely ass cheeks! The long leine, rather than hang loose, only moulded to his braies. This appeared to be the everyday fashion for the men, compared to the belt, hose, and doublet he wore at the wedding. Either way, he looked so dashing!

"You have a peculiar look on your face, dear. What is on your mind?" asked Nanny, who had come to her side.

"Oh, nothing, Nanny. Alex suggested we go and find Kenna to show us how we will spend our days."

"Your husband had no suggestions?"

"No, none at all," she said in a forced cheerful tone. "'Tis refreshing in a way, to have this freedom."

Saying the thought out loud gave her pause. She was

hurt and dismayed by the realisation that she may very well never belong here, if Alex's father's reaction to her was anything to go by. However, she still had something new here. She had found friends in Kenna and Izzy, and she now had freedom – a freedom she had never known, and suddenly everything felt lighter.

Linking her arm with Nanny's, she steered her towards the Great Hall. "Let us find out where Kenna is."

Chapter Six

They found Kenna tending her herb garden behind the kitchens, wearing braies and leine, just like Alex. Her hair was pulled back with a scarf, and there was a smidgen of dirt across her cheek. Back home, any woman of a certain standing would never be caught in such a manner, unkempt and doing menial work, but Grace found this refreshing.

Blushing, Kenna stood to greet them. "Apologies fer my appearance. I like to tend the garden daily," she told them.

"No apology necessary! In fact, I was just admiring your work. It actually looks enjoyable."

"Aye, 'tis. I find the feel of dirt and plants, living and breathing, verra calming. And I always feel accomplished after I do my tending," Kenna explained, pleasure evident on her face. "Ye can help me if ye like."

"That would be wonderful," Grace replied eagerly.

"We can start tomorrow. I should wash up and show ye around, as Alex wanted me to." Kenna washed her hands and face in the pail of water beside her. "Since we are out the back of the kitchen already, let us start there."

They headed towards the door, which was open that led to the cavernous stone kitchen that was bustling with more people then Grace could count. Fires with huge pots atop were being tended to and stirred. Tables had people chopping vegetables, preparing meat, kneading dough. Grace was fascinated by the amount of work going on which everyone performed so seamlessly.

"As ye can see, there is always work to be had, especially when Da is home. He is verra particular aboot meals coming out at certain times. A horn is blown twice a day to call everyone to the meals that take place in the Great Hall."

Kenna pointed to a couple working at one of the benches. The man was preparing some type of meat, which Grace guessed was a stag, going by the size of the hindquarters. The woman at the other end of the bench was rolling out dough.

"This here is Mr and Mrs Cook. They run the kitchens, so there is little need fer us down here. Mr and Mrs Cook, this be Alex's new bride Grace and her Nanny Bea." Grace and Nanny smiled warmly at the couple, and Mrs Cook returned a half smile while Mr Cook just grimaced. Grace saw Kenna's cheeks flush with either embarrassment or frustration, and followed Kenna as she signalled them on. There were others still to meet in the kitchen, but knowing they would take their leave from Mr and Mrs Cook, she did not want to cause further awkwardness.

As they exited the kitchen into the hall, Nanny Bea spoke. "They may not care for us now, being English and all, but in time they shall change their minds and see we are no different."

Grace knew that Nanny said this more for her well-being than for her own. Grace was not sure how she felt. Instead of the usual panic, she found herself annoyed. Not sure how to express the emotion, she just gave Nanny a smile and nodded.

"I am sorry Grace, and I hope it improves as we make the rounds," Kenna offered.

"Dinnae fash yerself, Kenna," Grace said with a Scottish lilt, causing Kenna to giggle. "'Tis no fault of yours how people act. And like Nanny said, it will get better in time."

"Ye have reminded me, Grace – I need to teach ye some words. Hmm, let's see ... What if we start off with yer name? *Is mise* Grace."

"*Is mise* Grace," she repeated slowly, and Kenna nodded enthusiastically in approval.

"Aye! Now to say 'good day', ye say *latha math*."

"*Latha math*," Grace repeated, this time with more confidence.

Once I build up enough knowledge and confidence, I will surprise Alex, she told herself, excited for the day ahead.

By the end of the tour, only Nanny still held a sunny disposition. Grace was cranky and Kenna fed up with her people. The miller, the smithy, laundry, chandlery, and so on, all either gave lukewarm greetings or outright hostile nods. Kenna was truly fed up by the time the three women returned to the kitchens for refreshment, and she berated one of the scullions. It was obvious to Grace that the man was put out when asked to assemble a tray for them.

"I will be telling Alex how poorly ye welcomed his new bride."

"What do ye mean, 'poorly'? I greeted her like I would any English person," he said indignantly.

"She is nae just an English person; she is yer future Laird's wife and now part of the MacNichol clan, ye great big *tolla-thon*," Kenna scolded, using one of Izzy's favourite expletives. Grace saw that the man at least had the decency to look slightly abashed.

"Come on, Grace, I saved the best fer last – the women's solar. Izzy has one at the Murrays' and I have been wanting my own, but 'tis nae fun alone."

Making their way into the keep and up the stairs to where Grace's and Kenna's rooms were, Kenna led them to a room right at the end of the hall. They walked into the room and Grace walked around in a circle. The room was spacious with a large window that faced the back of the keep, giving a view of the mountainous Highlands, and best of all, allowing the sun to shine through.

"'Tis wonderful, Kenna! This can be our solar! We will need to make some cushions and tapestries. And what a lovely space we have here to do so."

Nanny went to get their sewing supplies while Kenna and Grace arranged the chairs into a half circle. The fireplace held a pot, and Kenna had a stockpile of herbs, so they brewed some lemon balm tea. Soon the room smelt of citrus and was filled with a constant stream of happy chatter.

This is how Alex found them hours later – sewing and laughing. He was silent and didn't announce himself, and Grace caught him taking in the scene from the doorway.

"Alex, how nice to see you," she offered, a little awkwardly in her boldness.

"Aye, just checking in," he replied as he walked around the room, noticing the minor changes. "Kenna, how did the introductions go?" he asked, with his back to the other two.

Kenna looked to Grace, who held up her hand. "They were not very welcoming, if I am to be honest with you, Alex." Grace heard her own miffed tone, but was too incensed to care. She was gratified when he spun around in surprise.

"Dinnae fash, lass, I was gonna get to ye," he said, flashing a charming smile.

The full force of that smile directed her way was flustering. "Very well, but I am sure Kenna will advise the same."

"Grace is right, Alex. I was verra disappointed in many of our clan. They have Da's prejudices only, and have no reasons of their own," Kenna informed him indignantly.

"I will speak with them," Alex assured, his smile now gone and face serious.

Grace, knowing that settling in would be a difficult task, let alone having the clan forced into false kindness, shook her head. "I would prefer to just wait. I will just update you after we adjourn in the evenings."

Alex cocked an eyebrow at the intimacy this notion created. "I cannae work out if ye are as soft as a wee baby bird or as scrappy as a mad badger," he teased, making Kenna and Nanny Bea giggle.

Grace was wondering that herself. This journey had taken her far from a miserable place, and was bringing out new feelings. She found herself responding with moxie instead of angst; wanting to be heard instead of trying not to be seen.

I must be careful, lest I find myself overwhelmed as I was after the wedding.

As much as Alex irked her with his dismissiveness, he still made her feel safe, and with her new friends and medicinal arsenal she may find herself cured. Unaware she had drifted so deeply into her thoughts, she eventually heard Alex's voice saying her name.

"Grace, can ye hear me? I was just jokin' with ye, lass," he said, looking at her closely with a concerned expression.

She shook her head. "I am fine, I was just wool-gathering. But, now that you mention animals, I did not see any dogs around the keep?" Grace asked, quickly changing the subject.

Alex shrugged. "We have dogs, but fer hunting and the like."

"I have always wanted a dog," she said wistfully.

"Duff has a new litter of puppies!" Kenna said excitedly. "Can we ask Jamie and Izzy fer one, Alex?"

"Who is Duff?" asked Grace, at the exact same time as Alex was saying "nay bluidy way" to Kenna.

"Duff is Jamie's dog – a deerhound, huge and shaggy, verra sweet and protective and funnily enough, only afraid of Izzy's cat Freya," Kenna told her, giggling.

"Oh, he sounds lovely! And tell me of Freya," Grace urged, looking at Alex and unconsciously chewing her bottom lip. She may have a new feistiness, but she was still not going to argue with her husband's decision. But, a moment later, Alex made each of the women startle.

"Bluidy hell, we will get one of the damn puppies! I will send a messenger to Jamie now to find out when." He stormed out, muttering to himself about 'wiles' and 'lips'. Grace, Kenna, and Nanny Bea looked at one another and started to giggle.

"You are getting under his skin, love," Nanny tutted cheekily. "'Tis a good sign."

Women. What was Grace thinking biting her lower lip, her beautiful sad doe eyes gazing upon him? He had no choice but to agree to the damned dog. As he was looking for parchment, he started to laugh out loud to himself.

Married but one day and I have nae even bedded the lass, and she has me bending to her will.

It did warm his heart that Kenna now had a friend of her own station. And Grace, the sun streaming across her face in the solar, was radiant in her new surroundings. He felt his face spread into a smile.

Shaking his head in amusement, he did not hear his father enter the room and was startled to hear his voice. "What have ye got to be happy aboot, ye daft fool? Ye ken yer married to the English?" Out came the bitter tones.

"Aye, I am. And I dinnae want to have this conversation every time we come across each other, Da. It is what it is."

"Does yer English bride ken ye have bedded every lass from Glasgow to the Orkneys? She looks like a right English broad with a stick up her arse?" he sneered.

Alex sighed. "Da, I have been married one day. And nay, I am nae aboot to tell her. What purpose would that serve?" he asked, exasperated.

His dad just shrugged. "Once ye start playin' around on her, she will soon find out. Ye will never be faithful. Only thing ye have been good at is whorin' and fightin', Alex. I accepted ye fer that, but nae fer this."

Alex had hardened himself over the years to the mean-spirited remarks his father spewed out. But, this was a new insult, a new disappointment, and he could not help but feel a little pang of hurt. Not that he would let it show. "Och, Da, ye always ken how to make me smile. Now, if ye dinnae mind, I have a letter to write."

He felt his dad's stare on him for another minute or so before he heard his footsteps and the door open and close.

Mo dhia, Alex thought as it sunk in. *Life as I ken it is aboot to sorely change.*

The never-ending battle between the Scots and the English was apparently about to be played out in his own home.

Grace was panting as she tried to catch her breath, hiding in Kenna's room, the first room she had come across. She had gone to follow Alex after he left to thank him again for his kindness, and Kenna said he would be in his private quarters, the room close to the stairs before her own bedroom. As she'd neared the door, she heard the voice of Alex's father, which had stopped her in her tracks. The sound of his cruel voice caused that familiar feeling of anxiety to rise in her chest. Hearing what he'd said about Alex's debaucherous nature stung her, and it hurt more than the time she was actually stung by a bee.

That pain was sharp, pulsated hot, and began to itch. The pain she felt now was a dull ache in the pit of her stomach; she had just discovered that her new husband, whom she had felt so safe around, was a womaniser. Between the tight feeling in her chest and the ache in her stomach, she had not registered the blood pounding in her ears until

Alex's muffled voice penetrated her mind. She did not know she could even move that quickly, as the fight or flight response sprang into action. She had lifted her skirts for ease and ran to hide.

"What type of quagmire do I find myself in?" Grace whispered aloud to herself in despair.

She sat on the end of Kenna's bed and closed her eyes to focus on her breathing. She forced her mind to go blank for a few moments, to allow her heart rate to slow down and the tight feeling in her chest to ease.

I need to make a nice calming brew of chamomile.

Going to the door, she opened it slowly to peek outside to see if the hall was clear. Hearing and sighting no one, she dashed back to the drawing room.

Kenna and Nanny Bea's heads both bounced up in unison, startled at her devilish appearance. "What happened, child? You look a fright!" Nanny asked as she rushed over to her.

"Aye, what is the matter, Grace? Did ye find Alex?" Kenna's face was full of concern.

"Oh, oh, I am fine. Truly. I, I, uh ..." Hearing herself stutter, she tried to think of a little white lie. "Only, I heard your father, Kenna, and I decided to hide in your room till he passed, but then I missed Alex." It was not the truth but not exactly a lie, which assuaged her guilt a little. Nanny did not look convinced, able to see the signs when Grace had one of her episodes.

"Truly, all is well. Nothing one of those lovely herbal teas will not fix," Grace said, forcing a cheerful smile on her face. Kenna bustled away to heat some water over the fireplace. Nanny took up her needlework, still eyeing Grace suspiciously. Turning to face Kenna, Grace attempted a casual nonchalance with both her posture and tone.

"Kenna, I was thinking, there is so little I know of Alex. Was he ever married or betrothed?"

Kenna had turned to face her when she spoke, so Grace was able to see her cheeks pinken. "Nay, only ye," she said, before turning quickly to tend the tea.

"He is so very handsome, though. Surely there has been some young lady that caught his eye or that he dallied with."

"You are snooping, child. I knew there was more to what you said," Nanny whispered. Grace waved a hand for her to quiet, waiting for Kenna's response.

The tea finished, Kenna prepared the cup and walked over to her, looking uncomfortable. "I'm sure there has been, but Alex doesnae speak with me of such, sorry, Grace."

Thanking her for the cup with an apologetic smile, Grace felt guilty for badgering her. "I am sorry for being nosy," she said with sincerity. *It is not your fault your brother is a whoremonger*, she thought to herself, reserving her crossness for Alex alone.

"'Tis alright. Only natural fer ye to be curious," Kenna said with a wave of her hand and a small smile, which Grace understood as relief that there were no more questions. If Kenna did know of her brother's reputation, Grace understood she would not want to be the bearer of this news. She hugged her warm brew closer.

Chapter Seven

Alex watched Grace from the corner of his right eye as they ate their evening meal in the Great Hall. He watched her so intently that the raucous noise of his clan was a faded din as he wondered why his bonnie bride's nose was sorely out of joint. Her jaw was rigid, her posture tense, and she was shifted away from him. Her face was still set in that serene expression she wore so well, but he noted the slight crease in her brow like something was bothering her. And what all these signs told him – as a man, as a warrior, as a hunter – was that the woman beside him was greatly unimpressed with him. *Mo dhia, I have barely laid a hand on her, or spoken to her. Why is she so cross? Women.* With a shake of his head, he turned his focus back to the meal in front of him. The only bounty for this evening was his father was not here.

"Alex, ye look stressed; what is wrong?" asked Aran, who sat on his other side.

Not prepared for the question, Alex responded with a laugh before saying, "Stressed, me? Dinnae be daft, man –

ye ken little bothers me. I live life fer pleasure, nae fer stress."

A snort came from his right and he turned his attention to the source: his wife.

"That was nae verra ladylike," he said with a cheeky grin, glad to be getting a reaction even if he didn't know what the snort was for. Her face blanched as she turned to face him, and seeing how nervous she now looked, Alex felt guilty.

"You are right. I am sorry. May I be excused?" Grace asked, already halfway up. Before he could reply, Kenna stood up, too.

"I will come with ye, Grace," Kenna said, also throwing Alex a dirty look.

Dumbfounded, he turned to Aran again. "What in the holy rood just happened?"

"I am nae sure. She is a sensitive one, it seems," Aran replied with a shrug.

"Aye, but did ye nae see how rigid she was during the meal? That showed some spark."

"Nay, she is a quiet little mouse, but ye ken I was nae watchin' her as intently as ye." Aran was unable to contain his amusement at Alex's surprised expression.

"Aye, eat yer food, ye fool," Alex scowled, pushing himself away from the table. "Sorry state of affairs when a man cannae eat in peace." Alex ignored the guffaws of his men as he walked away.

Grace smiled at Kenna as she placed a hot, fragrant brew in

her hands. They were standing in her and Alex's bedchamber near the warmth of the fireplace.

"I do love this tea, Kenna. I really must thank Izzy again. It works miracles in settling my mind and calming the unpleasant fluttering in my belly."

"Ye ken ye dinnae have any reason to fear Alex," Kenna started awkwardly. "Aye, he doesnae have much tact, but he has a big heart."

Grace nodded, understanding Kenna wanting to defend Alex for his better qualities, and she sighed. "That is my problem. Alex makes me feel comfortable and safe, so I feel I can relax around him, but I am not accustomed to doing so." She was not able to continue explaining herself, as the door opened and Alex appeared, sheepishly looking from her to Kenna and back to her.

"Am I interrupting, lassies?" he asked, still standing at the threshold.

"Nay, Alex. I bid ye both good sleep," Kenna responded, giving Grace's arm a reassuring pat as she left the room.

Grace went to sit on the floor in front of the fire and sipped her tea, and heard Alex moving around the room behind her. His shadow fell across the floor as he came up behind her, and her pulse quickened. She gripped her cup tighter as he shifted to sit on the floor beside her. The room was silent except for his steady breaths, and her own which seemed loud and heavy. His hand stroked her hair before pulling a lock behind her ear, and the gentle touch made her shiver slightly, despite the fire that warmed the room. Turning to look at him, she saw him sitting by her side, his elbow casually resting on his knee as he eyed her with an expression both seductive and serious, firelight leaping across his face.

"What is wrong, sweet Grace?" he asked her, his voice sensually low. Not sure how to respond, she just shook her head, feeling like a silly dolt unable to string thoughts together. He started to stroke the inside of her arm with one of his fingers, and the warmth that spread through her from the sensation made it difficult to maintain coherent thoughts. "Talk to me, Grace. I want to understand ye, *leannan*."

The Gaelic word was foreign and intriguing, making Grace curious to find her voice.

"What did you call me – *leannan*? What does it mean?" To her surprise, his face reddened slightly like he had been caught unaware.

"'Tis just an endearment. But, I have got ye to speak to me, so dinnae stop."

"To be honest, Alex, I do not know how to explain it myself. My normal self has always tended to be ... reticent, but around you I find myself less so."

"Is that nae a good thing?" Alex asked, his tone now curious.

"I suppose it is, but I have not yet adjusted, and it makes my nerves a little frazzled," Grace said with trepidation, wondering how he would interpret this.

"'Tis good ye enjoy the brew of chamomile I think I can smell. I have heard Izzy and Kenna talk aboot how it is good fer calming." His reply was matter-of-fact, indicating no judgement or alarm.

"Then you do not find it odd that my nerves can get the better of me?" Grace hated how small her voice sounded as she asked, staring into her cup.

Alex caught her chin in his hands and gently turned her face back towards his and stared deeply into her eyes. His strong but gentle grip gave her no choice but to do the same. The kaleidoscope of blue hues entranced her.

"Grace, I dinnae think yer odd. I am nae judgemental or lack-witted. As humans we are all inherently different – the way we feel, react, and think. And that means some days, ye and I may fight or ye may think I am being a *bampot* or I may think ye are a pain in the arse," he said quietly, giving her a wink.

This response made her feel safe to share a little more. "It is something I work on within myself, and being here with you and meeting strong women like Kenna and Izzy encourages me to do so. Nanny has been my rock for so long, but in my father's home we both walked on tiptoes, not wanting to raise his ire."

"I have never been one to believe in fate, but aye, I am startin' to think there was a reason fer our sudden betrothal, and if that was to get ye away from yer da, I am glad. I am just sorry ye now have my da to contend with."

"Your father, while not the most pleasant, will be one of my challenges to face. I feel that as time goes on, I am going to become better prepared to fight for myself and not flee in fright and make myself small."

"I am yer husband now. Whatever stresses ye face, I am here."

His response left her in absolute awe. Who was this man? Philandering and insensitive, or loyal and gentle?

"Thank you," she replied, the two words the only she could manage. Her voice was choked with emotion, which she hoped conveyed how much she appreciated his words.

"Yer welcome," he said simply, with an easy smile. "But, tell me – was there anything else bothering ye?"

Unsurprised he asked, since he had expressed his keen

observations, she pondered for a few seconds whether she should tell him what she had heard, or if she let it be and not ruin this moment. She chose not to respond with words, closed her eyes, and leaned in close to press her lips against his. She felt his surprise, but he was quick to recover, returning her kiss with the pressure of his own full lips. Their sweet kiss quickly became heated as he encouraged her to open her mouth and his tongue swept in, stealing her last resolve.

The explorations of his tongue were thrilling, and he coaxed hers to become one with his as they entangled in a sensual dance. His kisses were varied, releasing her to take a breath before recapturing her lips, nibbling the top and sucking on the bottom. She felt herself falling deeper into this web of pleasure he was spinning, and he must have sensed the same as his hands moved to pull her over into his lap. He had refrained from touching her during their intense kisses, and the addition of his hands now added more devilment to the feelings stirred within her.

"I feel so alive, Alex," she said breathlessly, as he massaged her back with his hands as he peppered hot kisses along her neck. In response, he nipped the soft skin, the bite resulting only in pleasure.

"There is a fire inside ye, lass. One only I can stoke fer ye."

Standing, he scooped her up in his arms and walked towards the bed. She looked into his smouldering gaze and was amazed she had not disintegrated into dust, it was that fierce. They reached the bed, and he released her onto the furs. She watched as he removed his leine, the only thing he had worn. She had felt what she had assumed was his manhood when he pulled her onto his lap, but being so naïve, she did not think beyond it. Now, as he stood naked in front of her, she drank in his masculine beauty from head to toe, for his beauty definitely did not end at his face.

He was magnificent – not a word she had thought to describe a man. His skin was smooth, the hairs on his chest sparse as she took in the definition of the upper half of his body. She had already seen his arms were large, but the sinewy muscles not covered by clothing displayed his strength. Realising it was now or never, she dropped her eyes below to his manhood, but the large essence of him made her shy and she skipped straight to his large thighs that were a shade lighter than his calves and forearms. Then she heard his husky voice.

"Dinnae be embarrassed, *leannan*," he whispered, and something about this word bolstered her courage as she looked up to stare at the protruding flesh. Like everything else about him, it was large.

Intimidating, Grace thought, *but not frightening*. In fact, her curiosity piqued, and she heard his laugh again.

"Aye, I am glad ye are nae afraid; it will bring ye only pleasure, I promise ye. Now, my bonnie lass, show me the beauty under yer gown," he urged, reaching out to help her stand. Taking a deep breath, she first shook out her hair, the golden mass now behind her shoulders. She then trailed her fingers along the material of her gown as she hitched it up slowly, inch by inch. She was unable to look away from Alex's gaze, his pupils dilated and breath heavy as he focused on the patches of skin appearing as the gown lifted higher. In a second, it was over her head and at her feet. His expression was full of desire, and she watched as he stroked himself, his manhood looking even bigger.

"Ye are a goddess come to life. I dinnae ken how ye are real," he said breathlessly, still running his gaze over her. She imagined what he was seeing, familiar with her own body but never finding it that interesting. She had always thought she was a little plump and hippy, but her legs were long and lean and her waist small. She never paid attention to the fat she stored around her belly and bottom, but it appeared Alex was pleased. Her breasts, she thought, were just normal – not small, not big; and the hair on her womanhood was the same colour as her hair. She started to squirm under the scrutiny.

Alex noticed and spoke to her huskily, his brogue thicker than normal. "Sorry, *leannan*, I was caught up in yer spell. Come to me," he beckoned, extending his arms. She placed her petite fair hand in his large tanned one. He held her eyes as he drew one of her fingers into his mouth and sucked with a firm but gentle motion that sent erotic shots through her body. It intensified as he moved from finger to finger, amazing her that this act was causing so much pleasure. The trembling of her body was making it difficult to stand, and he took pity on her overstimulated state and drew her into his arms, giving her another soul-wrenching kiss as his arms caressed her naked body. He stopped and stood her in front of him again and she watched him drink in the sight of her, before lifting his eyes to meet her own.

"I want to ken every part of ye, Grace."

Chapter Eight

I n all that is good and holy in this world, how did I *deserve this fine specimen of a female before me?* Alex asked himself inwardly.

He had been with countless women. It was not as if he was overly picky, but he always looked for some beauty, and he had many a beautiful woman on his long list of conquests. What stood before him now, though, was something entirely different. He recalled his initial thoughts, when he pictured her as Aphrodite would look as she rose from the sea foam in all her glory. Grace's face, angelic yet alluring, evenly matched her luscious body. Her curves were plentiful to the point of perfection, encased like sand in an hourglass. The candlelight in the room made her smooth fair skin glow and haloed her golden hair. He drank her up with his eyes, and she wet her lips with her pink tongue, a nervous action but sensual all the same as it made him stir.

Och, I need to snap out of this trance. I must be making her self-conscious.

"Come to me, *leannan*."

As soon as the words left his mouth, she came and stood between his legs in an instant. She tentatively raised one knee onto the bed and leaned forward to place her palms on his chest.

"I do not know what to do," she whispered, her lashes fluttering down in shyness. He lifted her face to meet her eyes.

"Dinnae fash. I do," he whispered, and took her lips hotly with his own. He saw a brief expression of annoyance flash on her face, but he could not focus any attention on that as he ran his hands up and down the curve of her waist. Moving a hand to grip the back of her head and entwining his hand in her hair, he pulled her head to the side to allow him access to the elegant slope of her neck. Encouraged by her breathy sighs that escaped her as he kissed and sucked the tender skin, he moved down to her breasts, finally getting to feel the weight and shape of them in his hands. Kneading them gently he looked at her face and saw her eyes were closed, her cheeks flushed with passion, the colour deepening as he pulled at the hard tips.

"Yer passion sets me afire, *leannan*," he whispered in a ragged breath.

He gave her no option to respond with words, only with a moan as he took the pale pink tip of her nipple in his mouth. He felt her hands move to grip his head and the lower half of her body push forward against him, giving him the sweet victory of validation. He could feel the heat emanating from her as he moved to the other breast, to ensure it received the same attention. He rested her back, so she now lay on the bed, and he was on top of her. He moved up to take her lips again, kissing her with abandon as she writhed underneath him. He broke away from her mouth, needing to gain control of himself – something he never before had to do – and placed hot, wet kisses down her collarbone to her rib cage.

"Oh, Alex, I have never felt such bliss before. Please don't stop," she said breathily.

"Aye, and yer gonna get a hell of a lot more bliss before this night is over." His kisses were now on her belly as he dared to move lower. His new bride was proving full of fire and passion, not ice and prudence. He heard her surprised gasp of 'Alex', but she immediately opened her legs wider to accommodate him. He grinned as he positioned himself to pleasure her beyond any expectations. Making love to her in this intimate place, with his lips and tongue as he would her mouth, he felt a wave of possession flow through his heated veins. Encouraged by the movement of her hips and heavy breathing, he added his fingers to his repertoire, intent on making her climax. It was not long before he felt her body tense up and tremble and he was rewarded with the sweetness of her release. He heard her let out a little scream in ecstasy as her legs still trembled.

"Oh my god, oh my god. Alex, what was that?" Grace's blue eyes shone with awe as he looked up to meet her dazed gaze.

"That, my bonnie bride, is magic – the kind of magic only we can make together."

Moving his body up to lay against her, careful not to place all his weight on her, he grabbed her hand and guided it towards himself for her to clasp her hand around him.

"Are ye ready fer us to become one? I understand if yer afraid," he said quietly, realising she could now feel how hard and large she had made him.

"Yes, I am ready. I am not scared. And I trust you, husband." The lustful look he saw in her eyes emboldened her response and he prepared himself.

Take it slow, take it slow, he repeated in his mind. Never, ever was he out of control in these situations. He always held the power. But, at this very moment, he was hanging on by the thinnest thread. She was warm, moist, and holding onto his shoulders as he hovered over her and guided himself into her as slowly and gently as he could manage. This proved torturous, as he felt every exquisite moment of making her his, feeling her innocence become his as he broke through the barrier that only he would cross.

Watching every expression on her face, he saw the myriad of anticipation, awe, a twinge of pain, and then unadulterated pleasure as he chose a rhythm that had them both gasping for breath. Her dainty hands were now clutching his buttocks as she urged him to go faster, deeper, and that thin thread he was clutching broke as he spent himself inside her. The feeling of his climax felt somewhat different to previous times. *Aye, because she is so beautiful*, he told himself, but a niggling thought he ignored warned him it was something else. Needing to give himself some distance for a few moments, he untangled himself from her and saw she was lying there with her eyes closed, a soft smile on her face.

"Are ye alright, Grace?" he asked, checking on her as he got up.

"I am wonderful, husband," she said softly, eyes still closed. He grinned. For such an innocent lady, she had taken to lovemaking more eagerly than he would have guessed.

"I will get some cloth to clean us up," Alex said, seeing there was a little bit of aftermath of her chastity. "And then ye can tell me what ye enjoyed best, ye naughty wench," he teased, seeing her eyes pop open and her face redden.

Laughing at her sudden prudence, he walked away to fetch the cloths and some water.

"I think we are going to have many, many long nights, *leannan*, and long mornings. And sometimes, I may even have to steal ye during the day," Alex said, his eyes twinkling with mischief. Grace giggled and swatted his arm; he was incorrigible.

But, that innocent albeit impish remark led to a more dire thought. The magic of the evening began to dissipate as she remembered his reputation, and she felt the stirring of the tight feeling in her chest. She did not want to share what she had – the intimacy and closeness – with any other woman.

Can I trust that I will be enough for him?

"Why do ye look so pensive and unhappy all of a sudden, Grace?" he asked with genuine concern.

"How many women have you been with, like this?"

He sighed and turned his head. "Let me fix us a drink first."

Without any modesty, he got up and walked the room naked, fetching cups and ale and she watched him unabashedly. She would never have thought to call a man beautiful, but he truly was. No wonder he was popular with women. He came back to the bed and sat down, handing her a cup of what she sniffed to be ale.

"Why did ye ask me this?" he began, and she startled. She had been expecting an answer, not a question. Deciding only the truth would make this less muddy, she looked at him, then down at her cup, and back to him.

"I overheard a comment your father made to you today," she said without any guile, and he cocked an eyebrow at her.

"Ye were listenin' in on a private conversation I had with my da?"

"No! It was not like that. I accidentally overheard, and I did not announce myself as your father, well, he is ... you know ... and he makes me nervous," Grace explained, hating the stutter she heard.

"Dinnae fash, Grace, I ken yer meaning," Alex said, taking pity on her.

"And you are so handsome, you must have all the lassies throwing themselves at you." She tried to make a joke, but heard only jealousy in her tone.

He scowled. "I hate this 'handsome' shite. But, aye, I willnae lie to ye. I have had my fair share of women."

"But, how many?"

"I cannae give ye a number, lass."

"Is there that many? Is Scotland littered with broken hearts as a result of you?" she pushed. *How on earth did he not know a number?*

"Look, I may have loose morals, but I break no hearts. I tell the lassies upfront to have no expectations, as all I can offer is me at that moment."

"Oh, Alex, are you daft? As if they were not heartbroken. They get to spend an amazing time with you and know it will not happen again. You are not the most braw man in Scotland – you are the Highland Heartbreaker," Grace huffed.

"*Mo dhia*, whatever ye do, do nae tell that to Izzy. I will never live down the 'Highland Heartbreaker'.

"Is that all you have to say?" Grace pressed, her earlier nerves now turning snippy. He was acting so casual, and it was only making her ropable.

"Well, what do ye want me to say? I cannae change my past," he said simply and calmly, trying to placate her ire.

"And what of the future, Alex – our future?" His reaction made her heart drop. It was not a 'yes' or 'no', just a surprised look.

"To be honest, I havnae thought aboot it. This has been so quick, ye and I. I willnae lie to ye and make false promises just to make ye happy in this moment if I am nae sure I can keep it, Grace. But, after what we shared tonight, I am verra much pleased with our marriage."

Hearing his genuine and honest response, she knew it would be churlish to keep pushing for an answer. She knew that in most marriages, this was the norm, and a wife would never dare start this type of questioning. At least he allowed them to discuss it.

"Let us nae mar the night we have spent, *leannan*, with ifs and buts. Aye, come lay in my arms. I want to hold ye." She wanted that too, wanted that closeness back, and allowed herself to be wrapped in his warm embrace.

"Ye are a truly beautiful person, Grace, inside and out. Believe me when I say I will never intentionally hurt ye. My mouth may speak before I think, I may be hurtful, but I will do my best. This marriage stuff is new to me, as it is to ye," Alex said, pressing a kiss to her forehead. The simple gesture seemed to speak louder than the words and she snuggled against him, allowing the steady rhythm of his heartbeat to lull her to sleep.

BANG! BANG! BANG! The intrusive pounding on the

door awoke Alex with a sense of alarm, and he leapt out of bed and picked up his sword.

From behind the door came the belligerent tones of his father. "Alex, get yer arse out here! I wanna survey the lands today, ye ken!"

"Alex, what in the heavens is happening?"

He turned back to Grace, her blonde hair tousled and expression confused. Her altogether demeanour was tempting, and he only wanted to return to bed and ravish her.

BANG! BANG! BANG! "Did ye hear me, lad?"

"Aye, Da, I heard ye, as did the rest of the Highlands. Maybe even as far as the border," Alex said cheekily, winking at Grace's conflicted expression. It appeared that she did not know whether to be annoyed or alarmed.

"Bluidy smartarse," he heard his dad mutter, and he grinned at Grace.

"Appears I am needed to do my Laird-to-be duties today. Stay in bed. I will send a bath and breakfast up fer ye," Alex told her, thinking she may feel a little tender from last evening. "And I will send Kenna and Nanny as well." He picked a fresh leine and braies as he made his way to her side of the bed. Stroking her smooth cheek, he smiled at her sleepy eyes. "I will see ye later on today," he whispered, giving her a lingering kiss, unable to help himself.

Chapter Nine

Grace stared up at the ceiling and replayed the evening's events in her mind. She let out a soft sigh and asked herself how she had gotten so lucky. Growing up in a cold home and being betrothed to an even colder man, she never would have dreamed she would end up married to a warm man. Nor a Scotsman! She still had misgivings about his reputation and whether he would remain faithful, but she had a plan for the latter at least. *Keep the man's lust satisfied! Highland Heartbreaker indeed. Those days are behind him – he just doesn't know it yet.*

Giggling to herself, she imagined sending letters across Scotland to let the women know the Highland Heartbreaker was out of commission. Her thoughts moved to the morning's events and the abrupt awakening they'd received, and her good humour slowly faded. Alex's father was the only source of tension that made her feel angst. She dreaded coming across him alone. At least if she is with Alex or Kenna, she would feel safe, even if she still felt nervous. She looked over to where her pouch of herbs lay. They provided her comfort and a reminder of the progress she'd made in her self-growth journey. Thinking back to Ewan, his dislike for her, for her English ancestry, was palpable. And there was no remedy that came to mind as to how she could win him over.

I never won over my own father, she thought sadly.

Her father had found little use for her, except to marry her off. The man he had betrothed her to before Alex, a cruel baron, had made her father seem warm and fuzzy. A cruelness emanated from him; it shone in his eyes. Just the thought of him made her shiver and she pulled the furs tighter around her body.

A gentle tapping on the door broke her now intrusive thoughts.

"Grace, 'tis Kenna, may I come in?"

Grace welcomed her and moved to sit up so she could rise out of bed, but then let out a soft groan as she recalled she was naked and wrapped the covers even tighter. Clearly, lovemaking left one feeling a little worn the next day. Kenna came in, followed by servants with a bath. She saw Kenna look at the mussed sheets on the bed and felt her face pinken. Kenna must have had similar thoughts as her own face pinkened. Luckily, Nanny interrupted as she entered the room.

"Good morning, lovey. I bumped into your husband, and he asked that I bring you something to break your fast." Nanny's always cheery demeanour spread throughout the room.

"Thank you, Nanny," Grace said gratefully. "That was very kind of him."

"Wasn't it just, and he arranged you a bath as well, I can see."

"Yes, and I am looking forward to it immensely," said Grace, watching as the last of the bath was filled.

"I will leave ye to bathe, Grace. I just wanted to check in on ye. Meet me in the solar and we can decide what to do today," Kenna said cheerfully. "It is so nice having female company and being able to say that." Kenna left and Grace went over to the bath. She felt bold being nude, but she was eager to soak her body. Lavender had been placed in the bath and the soothing smell titillated her senses as she lowered herself into the warm water. Her tender muscles relaxed as the combination of lavender and heat soothed her. Nanny pulled a stool over to wash her hair. The familiar comfort of this routine they have shared many times made her feel calmer still. Unknowingly, she let out a long, contented sigh and Nanny's chuckle broke through her reverie.

"What is so humorous, Nanny?" Grace asked fondly, as she closed her eyes to allow the water to be poured over her head.

"It is just such a joy to see you at peace, dearie, and I dare say your handsome husband had something to do with it," Nanny finished with a cheeky wink.

Grace felt her face redden as she sputtered out a "Nanny," knowing very well what was being alluded to. Still chuckling, Nanny continued.

"Do not be shy. I may be as old as the hills, but I know where babies come from," Nanny said with a smile, causing them both to laugh. "But, truly it is such a joy to my heart to see you this way. The Highland air agrees with you, more so than the stifling English air that blanketed the moors."

"Yes, I am feeling a lot happier. I still feel the nerves, but they seem within my control. And if they do start to worsen, I have my herbal remedies. And Alex. He makes me feel safe in my body and I am hoping, in my heart."

"What do you mean by that, love?"

"He has flaws – flaws I am yet to reconcile."

"His father? I think his bark is worse than his bite. And Alex will not let him harm you," Nanny said reassuringly, massaging her scalp clean.

"No, not that. Well, yes, that. But also, I have discovered that my husband has a lusty past," Grace said, wondering how to politely say her husband is in fact a debaucherous fiend.

"Most men do, unfortunately. What is good for the goose has never been good for the gander."

"It's not that he has been with other women, it's more that he has been with so many, his face went blank when I asked him for a number!"

"That is odd bed talk between two newlyweds," Nanny said in confusion. Blushing, Grace realised how forward she must sound.

"I just do not like the idea of it, Nanny, or the idea that it might continue."

"I doubt it shall. Anyone with eyes can see the man is besotted with you. Oh, he tries to hide it to be sure, but it is there."

"I just feel like on one hand, I trust him with all I am, but on the other, I am seriously afraid he will betray me," Grace said, gnawing her lip.

Nanny patted her on the hand. "A life lived wondering what unpleasant thing will happen next is not a life worth living. You know this from experience, Grace. To be sure, I have heard the whispers around the keep that young Alex has had his fair share of women, but no talk whatsoever that one ever caught his heart."

"Oh, of course not! He is the Highland Heartbreaker!" Grace exclaimed, splashing her hands in the water, droplets flying from the tub.

"He is what?" Nanny asked, half smiling and half concerned at her impassioned display.

"My husband, Alexander MacNichol, is the Highland Heartbreaker. And I cannot ignore the tiny suspicion inside me that my heart may be the next one he breaks."

Alex realised he may appear like a petulant wee lad as he dragged his feet, and his sword, the sharpened point scoring the dirt as he followed his dad. They walked the perimeter of the eastern side of the keep which normally filled him with awe. From this side, the view was of the mountains. The impressive peak and rocky expanse seemed to go on and on like it never ended. It always made him feel small, which made him smile to himself since he was anything but small, and the beauty of it also gave him a sense of wonder. But, this was not going to be one of those days.

"Wipe that smile off yer face, ye daft fool. Ye look like a lovestruck lass," his dad berated him as he eyed him with suspicion. "Yer nae thinkin' of that English wife, are ye?"

Alex sighed. He had been thinking of Grace since they left. The feeling was maddening, like some kind of obsession. Sighting the mountains had offered him respite and he welcomed the momentary distraction. But alas, it was just like his father to ruin it.

"Well?" his dad demanded angrily, eyes still upon him.

"Nay, I was admiring our bonnie Highlands," he half lied, never having the energy to entertain his father's tantrums.

"Good. I brought ye out here to talk aboot this farce of a weddin' – I dinnae like it."

"Aye, ye have made that verra clear."

"Dinnae be a smartarse, Alex. I want to discuss with ye what we need to do aboot it."

"Do aboot it? She is my wife now, by order of our King. I cannae just turn her out," said Alex as his trepidation started to grow. *What is the man up to?*

"I ken ye cannae undo the weddin', but ye dinnae have to stay wedded, if ye ken what I am sayin'."

Alex stared blankly at his father for a few seconds as an array of emotions rushed through him. On one hand, he was shocked that his own father would suggest doing away with his wife. He also wanted to laugh at the ludicrousness that this was even a conversation. On the other hand, his protective instincts sent blood pounding in his ears, and he had to fight for control to not pick his father up by the front of his leine and toss him like a caber. Forcing himself to be calm so he could feign disinterest, he casually asked, "What do ye mean exactly, Da? Ye think I will set Grace aside and wed another?"

His father in turn looked happy with his response and nodded. "That's my boy. I ken ye would come to yer senses eventually, once ye saw what is between her legs is the same as any other lass, just English." Alex did not respond and bent towards the ground as if he was stretching to hide his expression, knowing one of distaste had spread across his face, and waited for his dad to continue. "She is a frail, useless lass. Whenever I look at her, I see a panic pass through her eyes. It willnae take much to do away with her. It just needs to be an accident, so no word of foul play gets back to the Bruce."

A red haze clouded Alex's vision as a drumming sound thundered in his ears. The very idea of losing Grace struck him deep inside, to parts he did not even know existed within himself. His father confirming the malevolent intentions he harboured was unconscionable. Taking a deep ragged breath in an attempt to steady himself, Alex searched for the words to respond. He saw that his dad had not even noticed his reaction as he stared off into the distance. *This is how twisted and selfish his mind has become. Hatred has gnawed away at his brain.*

"Turn around and face me," Alex said softly and firmly.

His dad slowly turned around, his expression surprised, but the mean glint in his eyes unchanged.

"Ye got something ye wanna say to me, lad?" Ewan's voice was also soft, though Alex heard the threat.

"Aye, I do. Ye will stay away from Grace, ye hear? She has done nothin' to ye, to anyone, and I have no interest in being rid of her. She is a quiet lass; she willnae be in yer way or cause any trouble, so ye can act like she doesnae exist. If ye hurt her, Da, mark my words, ye will rue it."

Alex spoke the words slowly and deliberately to ensure they were understood and penetrated. His dad's face flickered for a moment with surprise and disappointment before the usual sneer returned, his lips curled with disgust.

"Och, ye are a soft useless lad. It galls me to leave all this to ye," Ewan said, spreading his arms wide at the vastness. "And the half-bred whelps ye will spawn."

Alex folded his arms in a defiant pose, refusing to move an inch until he got some kind of assurance that his dad would back away from his scheming.

Spitting on the ground, his father gave him one more look of disgust before turning to walk away. But, before he took more than three steps, he turned back and spoke. "Fine, ye have my word I will leave the English lass alone. Just keep her out of my sight, ye ken? And later when training starts, I will handle the men myself. I dinnae need ye around."

Alex just nodded. He enjoyed the daily routine of training with the men, but he was happy to give his father the distance till he thawed out. And he was the Laird, after all; it fell to him to make these decisions. But, the decisions he made as Laird were starting to fill Alex with doubt. And the worst of it was, he did not know what he could do about it.

Chapter Ten

The following sennight was calm and joyful for Grace. Her days were spent with Kenna and Nanny busying themselves around the keep. She was learning new skills, things she thoroughly enjoyed, such as making candles. The more she worked about the keep, the more she found the people started to warm to her.

Now, Grace found herself without Nanny and Kenna as companions at this early hour; it was still dark outside. Her tummy grumbled and while it was still early for everyone to break their fasts, she wondered if she stole down to the kitchens if she would be able to locate something like fruit or bread to assuage her appetite. She was not familiar with the layout, and while the clan that worked in the keep were starting to warm up, there was still a slight barrier. She traipsed the stone steps so quickly that she soon found herself in the warmth of the kitchen. She saw Mrs Cook sitting by one of the fires with a large pot before her, cutting up parsnips, or white carrots as the Scots called them. She made a little 'ahem' sound, suddenly feeling like a naughty child, and Mrs Cook paused her chopping and glanced up.

"Good morn, milady," she greeted Grace, with a smile.

"*Latha math*," Grace replied nervously, testing out the Gaelic she was still not ready to try out on Alex.

Mrs Cook's smile widened, the skin around her eyes wrinkling in joy. "Aye, lassie, ye almost got that soundin' right. I am verra impressed."

Grace felt her cheeks pinken from the praise. "Thank you, Mrs Cook. Kenna has been teaching me, as I eventually want to surprise Alex."

"Well, ye can practise on me any time, lassie. Now what can I do ye fer? Ye hungry?"

"Yes, I am. Alex got up so early and I could not fall back asleep."

"Let me fix ye some warm porridge with drizzled honey and apple pieces. That's Alex's way of eatin' it."

She graciously accepted and sat down. Intrigued by this insight into Alex, she asked, "What else does he like to eat?"

"Och, the question should be what does that lad nae enjoy eatin'. He was all arms and legs as a wee lad, and forever stealing into my kitchens to see how he could fill his belly."

As they shared a laugh, more kitchen staff entered the cavernous room and looked at Grace and Mrs Cook in surprise. Feeling shy at the attention, she accepted the bowl of porridge placed before her and ate quietly as she observed Mrs Cook directing everyone to their tasks for the day. The warm porridge was delicious, the sweet honey and tart apple complementing each other.

Now that her tummy was full and the pleasant interaction with Mrs Cook still at the forefront of her mind, Grace headed to the Great Hall to help freshen the rushes and test out her newfound bravery of going it alone. The young lasses sweeping smiled shyly at her and she took this as a victory as she smiled shyly back. The time passed amicably as they spruced up the keep, a daily occurrence, and she overheard comments like, "She may be English, but she works hard," and, "She has a sweetness to her despite being English." Their slow acceptance of her had done wonders for Grace's nerves as she moved around with ease, and to make things even better, she had not once come face to face with her father-in-law.

Ewan appeared to be having his meals and sleeping elsewhere, and with that, he took the gloom of his presence. Thinking of how she spent her nights caused her to blush and she could not help but let out a soft sigh. Each night with Alex was magical as he took her to new unchartered heights of passion. The hot ardent kisses and knowing touches from his skilled hands – everything he did set her afire and she shed a layer of shyness after each night she spent with him. The only thing she could find fault with was they did not speak as much as she would like. She could see there was something playing on his mind, but whenever she asked, he gave her one of his irresistible smiles, those straight white teeth flashing in the candlelight. He would say "*dinnae fash, leanaan*" before dazzling her with his intoxicating kisses.

She thought it must just be Laird stuff, knowing he played a bigger role than he let on. His father seemed focused on the men only, while Alex managed the land, people, trade, and wealth. He came across jovial to all and like he cared for nought, but she now saw through that to the man he really was. He did not lead the clan by telling, but by doing. He ploughed the fields, worked with the horses, and one evening he came in blackened with soot as he'd spent the day with his blacksmith helping forge weaponry. When she compared it to the example of her own father, always ordering and demanding, it only deepened her respect for him as a man. His heart was good.

Grace looked up from the reeds she was preparing for the rushes in the Great Hall and caught sight of Alex coming towards her and her heart fluttered. He was the very definition of the word "braw" with his raw masculinity and handsome features. She saw he had a smile on his face and held a piece of parchment in his hands. Standing to her feet, she walked to meet him, laughing at herself as she tripped over her own feet in her eagerness. He laughed with her as he reached out to steady her, his long strides reaching her instantly.

"Och, my silly lass, ye almost fell head over heels," he teased playfully.

Head over heels in love, I fear, she thought to herself, slightly giddy as she felt his arms wrap around her waist.

"I have some exciting news in my hands. We are going to make our way over to the Murrays' fer a wee visit. Does that bring ye joy, *leannan*?" he asked, placing a kiss on the tip of her nose.

"Oh, Alex, that is wonderful news! I would love to see Izzy again!" She let out a little squeal as she hugged him, and he laughed.

"What can I say, I always aim to please."

"What is the ado about over here?" asked Nanny.

"Aye, ye two are looking verra happy," said Kenna as she joined them.

"We are going to visit the Murrays!" Grace told them excitedly.

"Oh, wonderful! Can I come?" asked Kenna eagerly.

"Of course," Grace and Alex replied in unison.

"Will Duncan be home?" Kenna queried with a blush.

"Nay, he is probably still completing tasks fer the Bruce."

"Does Jamie have any puppies left?" Grace asked eagerly.

"Nay, he would have found them all homes by now." He saw the disappointment on her face and felt slightly guilty. He then saw a frown furrow on her forehead and asked what was wrong.

"You know I cannot ride, Alex. Will I be a bother?" Grace asked, not relishing another ride in a cart.

Alex flicked his hand in a carefree gesture. "Och, ye will ride with me. Ye will be of no burden to my horse – ye weigh less than a fly that is always landin' on his back." This resulted in more giggles and Grace felt herself laugh.

Nanny interjected. "You will have to pass along my well wishes as I may sit this one out, Grace dear. My body is not ready for another journey that involves horses and carts."

"Of course, Nanny. You stay here and be at ease."

"Thank you, lovey. Come now, let us prepare packing for you and Kenna," said Nanny, bustling them away. She looked back at Alex. "And we will sort your things out as well, young man."

"Och, Nanny, ye are a keeper, ye are," he said cheekily, causing peals of laughter from them again.

Alex watched them walk away and sighed with a contented feeling in his chest. Since that despicable conversation with his dad, he had felt a little on edge, but could not help but lose himself in Grace's sweetness each night. He no longer felt that she had been thrust upon him unwillingly. She was his, his lover, his to protect from any harm. He just did not know how to express it in words, so he expressed it with kisses and his touch. He took more pleasure in her response than he did in the pleasure itself. There was such fiery passion underneath her veil of shyness that was slowly slipping away, and he revelled in it. Of most import, he had not come across any nerves or fear in her. Kenna let him know the days were spent harmoniously, and as he kept Grace close at night it seemed she was at ease. He took simple pleasure in holding her in his arms as she slept, and the steady beat of her heart and evenness of her breath let him know he was keeping her safe.

This trip to the Murrays' would be a welcome reprieve from his father. He had been walking around the outer area of the keep as he mulled over his thoughts, looking for Ewan to let him know to prepare the horses and supplies for a trip. He spotted Aran walking from the direction of the training grounds and hailed him over.

"How goes ye, Aran?" Alex greeted him, clasping his forearm with a firm shake.

"Yer da is working everyone hard today," Aran replied as he let go of the shake to use the back of his palm to wipe the sweat off his forehead. "Ye would think we are under attack."

Alex grimaced. "With his temper, we are lucky we are nae. The older he is gettin', the pricklier he is."

Aran nodded with empathy. "Dinnae fash; his bark has always been worse than his bite."

This did make Alex feel better, a reminder to not take his father so seriously. "Ye are right, Aran, that does bring me comfort. I have come to find ye as we are going to make our way to the Murrays'. If we can ready ourselves today, we will leave when dawn breaks. Get an early start."

"Aye, leave it with me. I will head to the stable now to pick the horses. How many of us?"

"I'm thinkin' seven. Kenna can ride herself, and Grace will ride with me," he said casually.

Aran grinned. "Wait till the lads hear this," he teased, drawing an eye roll from Alex.

"She has to come. I am gettin' her a puppy. 'Tis a surprise."

Aran, still grinning, just nodded.

"Now, I am gonna go tell Da my plans. I am sure he will be thrilled fer this respite," Alex said in a dry tone. He caught Aran chuckling as he turned to walk away. Aran had always been a good friend and Alex knew he would prepare things with Grace's comfort and safety in mind.

He heard his dad before he saw him, berating some poor lad for the way he was holding his sword. As Alex approached him, he plastered a smile on his face and reached out to the lad. "Och, lad, come here. I will show ye the best way to grip it so ye dinnae drop it," Alex said in an overly jovial tone, lifting the mood of the men who had been watching the flustered lad. They laughed and welcomed him, grateful for the distraction. Alex assisted the lad before turning to his dad, smile still in place.

"What do ye want?" his dad asked sourly with his arms folded over his chest.

"Just wanted to let ye ken I am takin' Grace and Kenna to visit the Murrays on the morrow."

His dad snorted. "To visit with that wildcat that Jamie married? Ye lads of today, got no bluidy idea what makes a good lass."

Alex smiled, but this time genuinely, as he imagined

what Izzy's spitfire response would be. "I quite like Izzy's spirit. But, like ye said Da, what do I ken aboot lassies?" Alex threw his arms out widely as he stated that last part loudly. The men guffawed at the comment as they thought of Alex's debaucherous reputation. His father had cottoned on to the joke as well and spat on the ground.

"There is yer problem right there, ye – bollocks fer brains." His dad now turned to walk away. "And good riddance to ye and the English lass! Give me some peace in my own home."

Alex winked at the men as he waved them farewell, except for Trevor and Stuart, two of his most trusted men, whom he called over to walk with him away from the group.

"Aran is preparing fer tomorrow, if ye both can lend him a hand. I will go round up Clyde and Garry to meet with ye, and we will leave at dawn."

The weather was kind as the day broke, brisk but bearable, and Grace rubbed her hands together for extra warmth as she watched the men bring out the horses. She watched with envy as Kenna went over to her horse. She saw her whisper something in its ear and the chestnut mare let out a snicker. Their bags and supplies had already been tied to the saddles, evenly distributed across the seven horses. Alex gestured her over to the huge black steed he and Aran stood near. It made sense that his horse would be large, considering Alex's own size, but she felt intimidated and a little wary of the imposing beast. Aran placed a fur over the saddle and turned to smile at Grace.

"Horse riding can take time to get accustomed to, milady. The fur will provide ye some comfort."

She offered a shy thank you, and realising he was referring to her bottom, felt her face flush.

"I am gonna mount up first, Grace, and Aran will place ye up behind me. Dinnae fash yerself," Alex told her with a warm smile, having sensed her discomfort.

Aran came next to her and placed his hands around her hips. "Okay, milady, I am gonna lift ye up, and I need ye to swing yer leg around the horse and put yer arms around Alex's waist."

She remembered seeing Kenna hike up her skirts and did the same, blushing furiously as her nerves began to kick in. She somehow managed to follow these instructions and before she knew it, was sitting behind Alex clinging tightly to him. The horse under her let out a snort, which to her ears sounded angry, and she began to panic.

"Be calm, Grace. He willnae hurt ye; I willnae let anything hurt ye. He is adjusting to the feel of ye, that is all. But if he senses ye are scared, it will make him scared." Alex's soothing tone and reassurance calmed her somewhat, and she closed her eyes and focused on steadying her breath.

"*Furasta, each dubh,*" he murmured to the horse, as he rubbed between its ears comfortingly. Grace felt the horse relax and she opened her eyes as her own tension eased. Aran was watching her with concern but not pity, and she smiled despite being caught in such a vulnerable moment, and he smiled back before going to mount his own horse.

"Let us be off. Clyde, I want ye at the front, then Aran on my left, Kenna to my right, and Trevor on the other side of Kenna. Stuart and Garry, ye will bring up the rear."

The men obeyed and started to move forward.

"Will there be danger, Alex?" Grace asked him.

"'Tis verra unlikely, but I like to be prepared. Are ye feeling okay? I cannae sense the jitters ye had when ye first got up, but if ye need a respite, speak up, ye ken?" As she couldn't see his face, she appreciated the gentle pat he gave her hand. She knew he said this with care and not as if she were being a nuisance.

"Thank you. I do feel much better. And I can see the change in your horse. He is strong and sure-footed, and I know I am safe with you." She snuggled her face into Alex's broad back. "But what is his name? I do not want to keep calling him 'horse'."

Alex cleared his throat and said, "'Tis *each dubh*."

"What does it mean in English?"

"Black horse."

Grace was silent for a moment. "Alex?"

"Aye, *leannan*?"

"I think it will be best if I name our children."

Chapter Eleven

The clip-clop of the horses' hooves mixed with the Highland sounds of the wind whistling through the tall pines and birches. The weeting of dotterels up above and the rustling of grouses on the ground built up the rest of the ambience. Alex was familiar with all these sounds he heard when he travelled away from the hustle and bustle of the keep. The foreign aspect of this journey was the dainty hands interlocked around his waist as he glanced down at Grace's smooth fair skin.

I should have gotten her gloves, he thought with regret.

Sighing inwardly, he shifted in the saddle. He still felt discomfort at times at the feelings Grace wrought inside him. The tenderness and protectiveness. The all-consuming lust, not only primal, but at a deeper level of emotional attachment he still was unable to fathom. He had imagined the intensity of these feelings would begin to ebb as time passed, but instead they continued to grow rapidly and he felt like he was losing himself – mind, body, and soul. His thoughts did not deter him from remaining alert and he looked around, scanning that all was well. It had been a few hours since they left and a rest for the women would be needed. Grace and Kenna had kept up an on-and-off chatter, but Grace had been silent for some time now.

"We will stop to rest soon, my well-travelled lasses. Nary a complaint from ye both! Yer arses are nae too sore, then?"

Kenna giggled and Grace let out a little gasp before reprimanding him with an embarrassed "Alex!"

"Och, milady, fer all yer husband's bonnie looks, he is nought but a *gàrlach*!" Aran called out in jest, and the other men and Kenna laughed.

Grace giggled as it was clearly humorous, and tilted her head back to ask Alex. "I suspect that was an insult at your expense, but pray tell, what is a *gàrlach*?"

"Ye were right fer laughin', and I ken ye will agree that I am nought but a rascal."

"Indeed, you are," she said playfully, and Alex felt her give him a squeeze. "But you are *my gàrlach*."

"If ye two get kissy, I am riding ahead," Kenna teased. "And I cannae wait to catch Izzy up on the miracle Grace has worked on ye. Yer table manners have improved, ye retire to bed earlier, and wake in the morn nae drink-addled."

This enticed more guffawing from his men. Alex had given little thought to Jamie and Izzy's reactions and grimaced as it now dawned on him that his best friends would rib him mercilessly.

"Alex, let us break by the clearing we are aboot to come upon," called out Aran.

Alex tugged the reins and steered *each dubh* to the clearing. There was shade and he heard the babbling of a small stream, a perfect spot to rest. Aran came over to assist Grace down and Alex dismounted after her.

"I am going to water the horses," said Aran, taking the reins of *each dubh* from Alex.

Kenna busied herself with one of the bags tied to her mounts. "I have apples and bannocks."

Satisfied, Alex turned to Grace, who was looking around curiously. "Are ye alright, Grace?"

"Oh, I am fine. I have not travelled much and 'tis nice being away from the busyness of the keep."

"Aye, it is much more peaceful," Alex agreed as he took a bite of a bannock and handed her one for herself. He watched her nibble at the hard flat oat bread, which was more like a biscuit. Simple fare, and not always very tasty.

He could not help but admire her resilient spirit, for a sheltered young lass. She did not complain or sulk at the arduous travel and meagre fare. She must have caught him staring at her, as she looked up and gave him her sweet smile.

"Do I have crumbs on my face?"

"Nay, ye are just perfect, Grace." Saying the words out loud gave him a sudden sense of longing – desperate long-ing. *She has every part of me in her grasp and she doesnae ken in the slightest,* he thought to himself, and he could not understand why this bothered him so.

Grace pressed her face into Alex's shoulder and gave thought to their travel. Aran had called out that they would arrive at Aberscross shortly, the Murray keep. Grace was unsure what had transpired to cause a shift in Alex's demeanour, but he seemed to have withdrawn from her. His movements were stiff and without affection, but his smiles and words still held a pleasant tone. The last two days of travel had become tiresome. Her bottom was stiff as she wiggled in the fur-covered seat, and she longed for a bath after the makeshift washes in the streams.

At night, she'd slept with Kenna covered in furs and under a drape for privacy. She and Kenna whispered and giggled until Alex told them to get some sleep, which only made them giggle harder, and this in turn got a heavenward 'mo dhia' out of him. Aside from this, she got little more from him. Determined to not let this change things between them, she nervously licked her lips, slightly chapped from wind and travel, and tried to calm the fluttering of nerves as she over-thought his behaviour. Before she spoke, it was as if Alex sensed her own sudden shift in behaviour and she felt him cover one of her small hands with his own large one.

"Is something wrong, Grace?" he asked, his voice low with concern.

"No, no, just excited and a little nervous I guess, to see Izzy again," she replied, feeling lame at her inability to speak honestly. She felt her nerves starting to grow. She did not want to undo the closeness and comfort that had sprung between them, but his sudden aloofness was making her question how strong it was.

"Are ye sure? I have felt yer breath quicken."

Taken aback, Grace could not help but pause for a few moments. It amazed her how attuned he was to her anxious feelings, but not to her annoyance at his inattentive behaviour. But, it gave her the courage to speak up.

Taking a steadying breath, she tried to look brave and attempted a casual tone. "I am just ready to be done with the travel, and have a bath and soft bed." She saw his eyes darken at her mention of a bath, and the smouldering gaze caused her belly to flip-flop. She mentally shook it off, not wanting to be distracted by his devilish allure. "However, Alex, while I have your attention, is there anything the matter with you?" She felt his own chest give a little jump in surprise at her question and it gave her a sense of satisfaction.

"Nay, 'tis just the travel. I need to spend my time being alert, ye ken; that is where I keep my attention." His tone now sounded unyielding and she decided to not push him further, realising there would be little point. *Funny, he does not raise my nerves, just my ire,* she thought wryly. In the distance, she saw the stone shadow of what could only be Aberscross Castle, the impregnable keep of the Murray clan. She heard Kenna give an excited cry and urge on her horse, and Aran quickly followed after her. Kenna's enthusiasm buoyed Grace's own.

"Faster, Alex, let us ride!" she cheered him on, excitement beating in her chest.

"Hold on tight, *leanaan*! *Each dubh* is aboot to show ye what he is made of."

Alex spurred his horse only to slow down when the Aberscross came into closer view, so Grace could take in its magnificence. He had heard Grace giggling and saw her arm waving at the villagers they had passed by. *Och, the Murray clan are welcoming her better than my verra own,* he thought to himself ruefully. Focusing his gaze on the keep, he pointed out the ramparts, the various buildings, and the spot where Izzy and Jamie had reunited.

Soon, he was entering the lower bailey and reining in *each dubh* as he spied Jamie and Izzy beaming at him with various Murray clansmen around them. Before he could turn to assist Grace down, she surprised him by leaping off the horse herself and bounding over to Izzy's open and eager arms. He watched Grace fling her arms around Izzy, being mindful of her much rounder belly, and Kenna joined them hugging and laughing. Little Jennet, Jamie's wee sister, was now introducing herself to Grace and to Alex's bemusement, Jennet gave him a look of ire before turning her attention to Grace in newfound adoration. Alex looked at Jamie who was shaking his head with mirth. Alex dismounted to walk over to him.

"Jamie, *mo laochan*, why do ye nae give me a greeting like this?" he jeered happily, holding his arms out wide. He would find out how he had miffed Jennet shortly.

"Ye are only a braw man to the lassies, Alex. I can keep my hands to myself," Jamie joked in return.

Alex quickly cut his eyes to Grace, worried that she would hear this remark and it would cause further discord between them. Luckily, she was absorbed in her women's circle and paid him no heed. Relieved, he turned back to Jamie and attempted to think of a witty retort, but upon seeing the look on Jamie's face he knew whatever jig he was about to present was up.

"Och, Alex, ye have fallen fer the English rose." Jamie's smile was wide and cocky. "And to think, ye were of little faith, with yer incessant whining! Didnae we tell ye it would work out?"

Alex scowled and brushed his hand through his hair. Before he could respond, he was again cut off, this time by the fiery-haired Isobel who was eyeing him and her husband with suspicion.

"I ken there is something afoot. Usually ye are the one scowlin', Jamie, and Alex has that silly look on his face."

"And hello to ye as well, sweet Isobel! How I have missed yer charmingly quaint ways," Alex drawled in exaggeration, giving her a deep bow.

Izzy scoffed, but held out her arms for a welcome embrace with a cheeky warning. "Dinnae squish my belly with yer brutish strength."

Giving the wee termagant a gentle hug, he decided it was the perfect time to move the conversation forward and away from his own behaviour. "Ye ken I have been looking forward to the famous Murray hospitality, and the famous Murray bathing room."

The hospitable hostess in Izzy kicked in instantly and she began to wave her arms, ushering them towards the entrance of the Great Hall. "Aye, and what a treat we have in store fer ye both. Guess who has stopped in fer a visit?" Before anyone could even venture a guess, Izzy blurted out with joy, "Arliss, the great *seanchaidh*!"

"What does that mean, Izzy?" asked Grace curiously.

"'Tis our word fer storyteller. Arliss is well-travelled and learned, and his stories are filled with adventure and wisdom," Izzy replied.

"Oh my, that sounds wonderful! I cannot wait to hear his words."

"I have planned a great feast fer this eve. We shall be merry and celebrate!"

Kenna and Grace clapped their hands together and began to discuss their clothing for the evening.

Alex turned to Jennet and knelt down so he could meet her height. "*Latha math*, my wee bonnie Jennet. Seems I have wronged ye, as ye havnae smiles fer me?" he asked her in an earnest tone.

"Ye didnae invite me to yer weddin', Alex. 'Twas verra rude of ye," she replied, disgruntled, her arms crossed.

Holding back laughter and keeping his face serious, he grabbed her two small hands. "Ye ken I didnae mean to hurt yer feelings. It all happened verra fast with little time to invite anyone." To be fair, it was Jamie's decision not to bring her, but Alex could not resist placating her.

Jennet unscrunched her face and beamed one of her big smiles. "Aye, I ken, and I really like yer Grace, she is so verra bonnie and kind! Ye just remember to invite me when yer bairn comes."

Alex choked a little and he heard Jamie laugh. "Do ye ken something I dinnae ken, Jennet?"

Jennet shrugged. "Jamie and Izzy got married and *poof* – a bairn is on its way. So, this means ye get married and ye get a bairn. I willnae get married fer a verra long time. It happens so fast."

Alex was left speechless, thinking of no way to respond, and Izzy came to his rescue. "Come, Jennet, let us go ready ourselves fer the feast. We ladies will bathe now. And one day when ye are a wee bit older, I will explain to ye how bairns and marriage work." Izzy, unflappable as always, was in contrast to the reddened faces of Grace, Kenna, and even Jamie.

As the women walked away, Alex chose this moment to get his dig into Jamie. "I am glad that awkward moment wiped that smirk off yer face. Ye ken young Jennet will be askin' ye and Izzy questions now till she gets answers."

Jamie grimaced. "Och, I will leave that to *mo aingeal*. It is a lass's duty to explain that."

Alex raised one of his brows, the dark hairs matching the hair atop his head. "I will remember to mention that to Izzy next time ye vex me. Ye ken she will give ye what fer."

Alex and Jamie reached the Murrays' Great Hall, bantering like young lads. They sat down and Jamie hailed a servant to bring refreshment. It was fairly empty at this time while everyone was out and about doing their tasks, except for Alex and Jamie and some of the men who were seated further away, talking amongst themselves.

"Now, tell me – how is everything back at home, with Grace and yer da?"

Alex filled him in on everything that had transpired with his dad, and watched his friend shake his head in disbelief.

"I ken yer da has issues, but that is too much, even fer him. Is this why ye want a pup, to protect her?"

"Aye, I guess it will be a protector. But, she mentioned it to me, and I want to make her happy." The words echoed as he saw that frustrating grin spread across Jamie's face. "Fine, I confess, I like my wife – are ye happy now?"

"Aye, I am," Jamie laughed. "And what of her nerves? Izzy mentioned it to me."

"There have been moments, but overall, when I see her eyes start to widen in alarm and her breath hitch, I watch her calm herself. She is a tough lass, tougher than she even realises. I find myself attuned to her nerves and body language most of the time, and she enjoys drinking her herbal teas and having the herbal baths Izzy recommended."

A cackling suddenly echoed through the Great Hall. Everyone turned to see Morag, a healer and wise woman, and the Murrays' *seann bhuidseach* (much to Jamie's consternation). Alex grinned at Jamie who held little patience for magic which he viewed as nonsense, and Morag took joy of her own in his displeasure.

"What brings ye here, Morag?" Jamie asked.

"I am here to see yer bonnie wife, milaird," she announced, giving one of her smiles that highlighted her many missing teeth. "And I cannae but help hear that Alex the Braw, lover of lassies all over Alba, has fallen so daft over a *Sassenach*."

Alex saw some of the men trying not to laugh and raised his hand in a dismissive gesture. "Och, aye, I care fer my English bride – let us all laugh and be done with it. Morag, 'tis nice to see ye," Alex said, giving her a polite nod.

Morag gave him a solemn nod in return. "I will find ye at a different time. I have something to tell ye."

Alex turned to Jamie who gave a long sigh and said, "I wish ye luck, my friend."

Chapter Twelve

race was charmed by wee Jennet, such a bright and curious child, her cheerful nature infectious. Jennet was currently pulling her towards the stables, saying she had a surprise for her.

"Hurry, Grace, ye are gonna be so happy with what I have to show ye," she eagerly told Grace as she tugged on her hand.

Izzy and Kenna were following behind them chatting, when Izzy must have caught wind of what Jennet was saying. "Jennet, the surprise is nae from ye," she admonished lightly. "'Tis from Alex."

From Alex? She knew they were headed to the stables, but Grace was nonplussed, not being one for horses. Now she was confused. "A surprise from Alex in the stables, how very curious," she murmured.

"Aye, but I helped pick the surprise," Jennet interjected.

"Och, ye cheeky little imp! Grace gets to choose her surprise," said Izzy with a bemused shake of her head.

"Oh, heavens, is the surprise a horse?" Grace asked nervously.

"Nay," said Izzy and Jennet in unison as they arrived at what could only be the stables, as Grace inhaled the smell of hay and manure. She could hear Alex's voice coming from within but could not make out the words. Jennet let go of her hand and ran past her into the stables, yelling out their arrival. Alex came to Grace and took her hand and guided her in, looking shy and vulnerable, a side she had not yet seen, and she felt her heart expand.

"Oh, Alex, what is it?" she urged, squeezing his hand as he guided her towards the back of the barn. She could hear yipping sounds and looked around at the horses, knowing they did not make those sounds. Alex suddenly let go of her hand and stood behind her, placing one hand over her eyes and the other on her lower back as he navigated her into a stall.

"I remember what ye wanted, lass, and I lied to surprise ye instead," he whispered in her ear, his hot breath against the nape of her neck sending a tingle down her spine. He lifted his hand from her eyes, and she was greeted with the joyful sight of a deerhound and her pups.

"Oh my goodness, Alex! I thought there were no pups available!" Grace squealed in delight as she dropped to her knees. "Look at this sweet precious family!" The pups, excited by the attention, ambled over to her as their mother watched on keenly.

Jamie dropped down beside Grace and patted the mother of the pups on the head. "Dinnae fash, we are keeping yer wee babes in the family," he said in a soothing tone.

Alex cleared his throat. "*Babe*, Jamie. A pup. *One* pup," said Alex, but when Grace looked up she saw the twinkle in his eye. She smoothed the soft fur of each pup one by one as they sought her attention. There were four in total, and she saw that there was a smaller one, who kept being pushed to the side by its siblings and those big brown eyes were beseeching her for attention. She leaned over and picked up the pup and love exploded within her heart as she cradled the ball of fur.

"That is the one fer ye, Grace," said Izzy with a happy smile.

"That is a lass ye got there, Grace. She is the runt but will grow big and strong, just like her parents," Jamie assured her.

Grace had never had something to protect and defend before. This pup filled her with a sense of purpose, and she looked up to the man who had organised this for her.

"Thank you so much, Alex. This is a most happy moment for me."

Before Alex could respond, Jennet spoke up. "Happier than yer weddin' day, Grace?" she queried innocently, causing everyone else to laugh.

"No offence to my dear husband, but much happier indeed."

Alex sat at the main table in the Great Hall and felt conflicted. Contentment and restlessness wrestled within him. The raucous celebrating Murrays that surrounded him could not even distract him from these feelings. On one hand, he was content that Grace was happy – happy to be with the Murrays, and happy with her new pup she had named Boudica.

Boudica was named after the Queen of the ancient Iceni tribe who battled the Romans invading Britain, which of course Izzy, Kenna, and Jennet just adored hearing about. A strong female warrior was Boudica, and her spirit seemed to live on in the women in his life, Alex realised as he smiled fondly.

But, something inside him was restless. He had not been intimate with Grace in what seemed like forever, and while he found himself pining, she seemed unbothered.

And it bothers me that I am so bothered that it does nae seem to bother her as much as I.

Realising how idiotic he sounded, he took a swig of *uisge beatha* and called himself a *bampot* as he stared out across the room. He saw a figure in the doorway and strained his eyes to see. He could feel whoever it was staring at him, but the shadowed figure moved away before he could make them out. He felt a nudge of an elbow into his arm.

"What is brooding, Alex?" asked Jamie.

"Aye, dinnae fash, I am in a rotten mood."

"Well, Arliss is aboot to tell his stories. That will liven up yer spirits!" Jamie said assuredly, as he gestured for the well-travelled man who sat across from them to stand. Jamie also stood and cupped his hands to his mouth, his voice booming over the din of the clan. "Let us all be quiet and turn our attention to Arliss, one of the special guests we have among us tonight along with the MacNi-chols, who will enrich us with his tales of yore and beyond."

Alex observed Grace's rapt interest as Arliss took to the middle of the Great Hall, smiling and waving. His long beard was now a faded red and swung to and fro as he moved his arms. Alex sensed the feeling that he was being watched again, but as he scanned the room, he could spy no one. Someone had blown out some of the candles and the room had dimmed, to create an air of mystery, but he felt an unease.

Arliss cleared his throat and began a tale of the Battle of Dollar, a bloody fight between invading Danish and the men of Alba led by Constantine I. Alex soon found himself immersed in the tale and like any other hot-blooded Scot in the room, got swept up in his own imagination of fighting in the battle alongside his ancestors. Finally, Arliss slowed down his storytelling and asked everyone to heed his next words.

"I have a tale fer ye – a tale of wisdom and foresight. Listen carefully as I say the words and let them sink deep into yer mind."

A ploughman was confined to his small farm due to bad weather, and he was unable to go out to find some food. So, he first ate his sheep, and as the bad weather persisted, he next ate his goats. Eventually, as there was no respite, he turned to his oxen. Seeing this, the farm dogs said to one another:

'We had better get out of here. For if the master eats the oxen, we're next!'

"Heed these words." Alex jumped in his seat at the eerie warning. The raspy voice, and unwelcome breath on his neck were unexpected. He turned around to see who it was and came face to face with Morag.

"Morag, why are ye sneaking up on Alex like that?" Izzy laughed. "Come meet his bonnie bride, Grace."

Arliss had finished his bout of entertainment and the Great Hall was filling again with talk and laughter. Alex watched Morag meet Grace, still annoyed by her abrupt and strange behaviour, and frowned.

"I have seen so many sour faces from ye today, Alex," Jamie said, as he bit into an apple. "What is yer problem, now?"

Alex scowled. "'Tis Morag and her riddles. Why is she telling me to heed Arliss' words? What did that tale even mean? I am no farmer that ploughs."

"'Tis the hidden meaning; the story within the story; the moral," Jamie explained.

"Aye, but what is it?"

"Ye are to be careful, Alex. Be careful of anyone close to ye that wishes harm to anyone else close to ye," offered Morag, who had again appeared behind him.

Alex turned his body in full and tried to dazzle her with one of his most charming smiles. "Och, Morag, would ye like some ale? Join us and tell me what ye mean!" He encouraged her, extending an arm to the table, hoping to charm some clarity from her and whatever the hell she was talking about.

Morag just cackled. "Yer braw and bonnie looks dinnae work on me, lad."

Grace leaned over his shoulder and smiled at Morag. "You are as wise as Izzy tells me, Morag, especially if you are immune to the charms of the Highland Heartbreaker."

This comment drew another raspy cackle from Morag. "Ye have a good spirit, lass. Keep it strong and stick close to yer husband."

Grace smiled sweetly, not understanding that everything Morag said had a double entendre, and not always for the best. Not wanting to discuss this any further with Morag in front of Grace, Alex tried another tactic.

"Come now, Morag, *mo chridhe*. Do ye need someone to escort ye safely to yer hut this eve?" He knew she had a hut in the woods behind the keep.

Morag shook her head. "Nay, but ye can accompany me to the bailey – give the lassies something to whisper aboot, seeing Morag the *seann bhuidseach* on the arm of Alex the Braw."

Alex sighed in agreement and stood and proffered his arm to Morag and looked back down at Grace. "I willnae be long."

Alex, accustomed to his usual long stride, had to take smaller steps to keep in pace with Morag as they walked across the Great Hall in silence. He sensed she wanted to wait till they were outside to give him her message. As they stepped into the cool and brisk evening air, she curled her finger at him with a gesture to bend his head towards her. Alex did so without question and waited for her to speak.

"I have read the ancient runes. They tell me their own story. A story of new life and life lost. I sense betrayal; I sense protectiveness fer those ye love. Arliss' stories, like my runes, have purpose and are told fer a reason. Something follows ye, Alex – ye and Grace – some of it good, and some of it bad."

Alex felt the heaviest of stones sink into his stomach. *What does this all mean?* He ignored the other little voice that told him he knew who this must relate to.

"Can ye tell me who I must watch out fer, Morag?"

She shook her head. "I cannae see who it is, or what it is. I can only caution ye of what I ken."

Alex nodded his head in acceptance. He was aware of how anything magic and otherworldly worked; his mother had always held a deep interest. You had to take the information as it was and interpret it in a way you thought was best.

"I will leave something in yer room fer Grace before ye depart," Morag said, and with a few steps she disappeared eerily into the night, leaving him only with unease.

All he wanted to do was hold Grace in his arms, to lose

himself in her ardour. He headed back inside, and an idea began to take shape in his mind as he searched for Izzy. He found her speaking with some of the clanswomen and gestured her away. He needed time with Grace to think of nothing but themselves, even just for a little while, to distract him from his thoughts.

"Aye, Alex, what do ye need?"

"Do ye think ye could arrange a bath fer Grace?"

Izzy raised an eyebrow. "Aye, of course, but she did wash earlier. I had water brought to her room to give her some privacy and am yet to show her the bathing room." Izzy eyed him suspiciously. "This is nae just a bath fer Grace, but fer yerself as well," she realised, rolling her eyes. "Devilish rogue. Aye, I will arrange it fer ye. Only because ye look so embarrassed."

"I am nae!" Alex protested, but she shushed him.

"Alex, trust me when I say it is nice to see yer softer side because I can assure ye, sleeping yer way all over Scotland is nae so cute. Leave the plans to me. I will signal ye when to take her up."

Chapter Thirteen

race wondered where Alex was taking her. It was getting late and she was exhausted, but he seemed very eager so she could not help but indulge him, wherever they were going. He had not been himself the last few days, but whatever it was he seemed to be shaking it. She held his hand as he guided her through the keep. The tallow candles that lit the way were dim as they had melted almost to the stub. It created a romantic ambience as he guided her towards what he was calling a surprise. They stopped at a chamber door, and he turned and gave her a toe-curling kiss before giving her one of his slow, sexy smiles.

"I have a treat fer ye, *leannan*." His whisper was like a soft caress as he opened the door and led them into a room where the candles were now brightly lit. In the middle of the room was a large bath, large enough that her first thought was lustful with the realisation they would both be able to fit in it. It was filled with water and dried herbs she recognised as lavender which emitted a calming and floral scent, enhanced by the warmed water.

"What are ye thinking?" he asked, sounding a little unsure.

Grace realised she had been standing there in silence, staring, and her face heated with a blush. "Oh, it's beautiful, Alex. Thank you for being so thoughtful. You certainly are surprising me. I feel so very cherished – thank you," she said with a smile, giving him a shy kiss on the cheek.

The candlelight bounced off the stone walls, creating a romantic ambience. She saw his eyes were locked with her own, and they darkened as sensuality swirled around them. He didn't use words to respond, but pushed the sleeves of her gown off her shoulders and pulled at the ties around her waist. She felt as if she were in a trance and before she knew it, she was standing there naked. His hot gaze perused her body from the tips of her toes back up to her eyes which he again locked with his own. Her pulse quickened under the intensity of his gaze, but the reaction it caused in her body was not the frazzled nerves of a spell, but the lusty anticipation of knowing what was to come. Emboldened, Grace reached towards him and pulled at his leine.

"Now, it's my turn to undress you," she said lowly, surprised to hear how sultry her voice had become.

Alex gave her a slow, wicked smile and lifted his arms up over his head, allowing her free rein to pull up his leine and turn downwards to pull down his braies. Her breath became heavier as she saw the result of his passion rise. Continuing on her emboldened path, she resisted any shyness and reached out to feel the hardened proof of his arousal. She could tell he was enjoying her confident attention and heard him let out a deep contented sigh.

"Get to ken me, *leannan*. Touch me wherever ye want," he said breathily, his brogue thickened in lust. She began to stroke him, gently at first, but became firmer as her confidence grew and she saw him enjoying her attention. His hips bucked towards her as his pleasure increased, which excited her and she felt the telltale signs of her own arousal. Grace's skin was flushed and tingling, and she felt the moisture between her legs.

"Ye are becoming quite the seductress, *leannan*," he said huskily. "But, I dinnae want to spend myself until I have more of ye." He drew her into his embrace and kissed her deeply. Grace wrapped her arms around his neck and held him for balance as he took her breath away. She felt him lift her gently and walk back where he placed her in the warm scented water. She moved back as he stepped in as well and sat down.

"Come sit between my legs, but face away from me," Alex beckoned. She did what he asked without any question, settling back into his large chest, the sparse hairs tickling her back. She watched his hand dampen a cloth in the water and he had a bar of soap in his other. He began to assault all her senses at once as he pressed warm kisses and soft bites against the nape of her neck, and used the soap and cloth in unison on her body. The feel of the soft cloth and silky soap massaging her skin sent erotic charges through her. He gave her no quarter as he touched her breasts and the now throbbing need between her legs, and she gripped his thighs tightly as she squirmed and moaned in delight.

"Oh, Alex, it must be a sin to be made to feel this good," Grace managed to say, gasping as he pinched one of her nipples between the wash cloth.

"Nothing we do is sinful, Grace. But, I will agree to it being verra, verra wicked, and if that makes me a sinner, then I will happily make my way to the fiery depths of hell," he said lustily, as he rolled her hardened nipple between his fingers.

She could feel his arousal, hard and big pressing into her back and she could not wait any longer to touch him. She turned around, the water sluicing over her body, and straddled him while cupping her hands to his cheeks. For a moment, they said and did nothing. The only sound was their heavy breathing and the water that rippled with any slight movement. It seemed a transcendent moment as their eyes collided and she saw deep into his soul. She saw happiness and lust, but she also saw fear. She saw love shadowed in his blue irises, but before she could explore what he feared and if that truly was love, she saw he broke their gaze.

Alex swept her lips in a fierce, almost aggressive kiss. But, the aggressiveness only inflamed her need as her tongue met his own just as fiercely. His hands were between her legs and he stroked her inside and out till she broke free of his kisses to cry out in euphoria, as the shuddering waves of her release flowed over her. Before she had any chance to recover, he lifted her hips and pulled her forward so she now sat astride him, and he slipped himself inside of her in one stroke. This pose was different from their previous lovemaking, but she embraced the unknown and let instinct take over as she began to gyrate. She watched his expression, eyes closed and mouth open as he groaned deeply, and she knew this was what he wanted. The position and angle was also stimulating for her own pleasure, and she enjoyed the power of controlling the depth and intensity of the penetration. She looked at him again and found he was watching her with a slow, sexy smile.

"Ye amaze me, *leannan*. Yer fire and passion – give all of it to me," he told her and gripped her hips even tighter. He bent his head to suck her nipples and the additional sensation made her move faster and she began to feel the shudders in her body rise again as she reached another peak. She lost all sense and control of her mind; all that she felt and all that mattered in this moment was her and Alex and their bodies joined as one. They were both breathing heavily and panting, and Alex gave a deep groan as she felt him spill his seed inside of her. This set off her own orgasmic spasms rippling through her body, and she bit his shoulder, worried her scream would be heard throughout the keep.

Her body felt limp as the aftermath of her release faded. It had sapped her of all energy. Their chests were pressed to one another as they embraced, and the fast beating of their hearts seemed to echo throughout the chamber.

Alex broke the silence first. "I will cherish this night fer all my days to come," he whispered, as he gently kissed her forehead.

"As will I. For a few precious moments, it is like the world is reduced to just you and I."

The energy in the room was full of contentment and satisfaction, and she hated to potentially ruin the moment, but she felt so close to Alex right now. For a moment during their lovemaking, she even thought he was going to say 'I love you'. The nerves that seemed to always lurk down below in her psyche started to stir.

"I hear the wheels turning in yer head, Grace," he said, his lips curled into a smile. "Dinnae fash on yer own – share it with me."

She sighed as the nerves instantly calmed, grateful that for anything else that may not be ideal in their relationship, his reassurance always made her feel at ease.

"I was just thinking that on this journey, you seemed at times not yourself, is all. I cannot help but wonder what is wrong," she said quietly, staying bold and watching his face as she saw his look of surprise.

"Och, when I travel outside MacNichol lands I need to remain vigilant, especially when I have such precious cargo," Alex said, flattering her as he nuzzled her neck.

"I was worried I had done something wrong, but I could also sense that whatever was on your mind, it was *not* that I had done anything wrong. I just want you to know you can talk to me, Alex." The last bit came out in one big breath, lest she be too bold.

His expression gentled and he tucked a long lock of hair behind her ear. "I ken that, Grace, and ye can always talk to me as well. Sometimes with me, I will have men stuff on my mind – like keeping ye and the clan safe, or things that need to be done on the land. I dinnae need to bore ye with that. I also wanted ye something fierce while riding that horse, yer bonnie curves pressed up against me, and I had to control my heartbreakin' ways."

She attempted to laugh throatily like a temptress, but was unable to pull off the saucy reaction and giggled instead. The water had cooled, and the fire was dying, and she gave an involuntary shiver and burrowed close towards him. "That would not bore me. Plus, I tell you what us women do – the sewing and mending, the tending of the plants."

"Aye, but that is riveting stuff. Of course I wanna ken that Nanny mended my leine and that Kenna stepped in horse shite," he teased, drawing a giggle from her with his cheeky remark. "But, 'tis getting cold now, my sweet Grace. Let me dry us off and dress so we can go to bed."

Like a wee babe and still too languid to move, she allowed Alex to lift her from the bath and stand her in front of the dying embers of the fire as he quickly dried her and then himself with a drying cloth. She giggled as he pulled his leine over her head and pulled on his braies only, with everything else under his arm as he guided her out. She held the candle as he whispered directions back to their chamber. Once inside, he went over and stoked the fire and ordered her to jump under the covers, lest she catch a chill. She kept his leine on, enjoying his heady scent, and watched as he placed things away. His back was to her, and he was pantless so she admired his toned bottom, but was distracted when she heard him curse.

"What is wrong?"

"Aye, nothing. I just pricked my finger on a brooch."

He shuffled around for a few moments before heading over to the bed to slide in beneath the furs. Curling her up against his body, he whispered something Gaelic to her and closed his eyes. Sensing how tired he was, she made a mental note to ask Izzy what the words meant tomorrow and closed her own eyes. *Mo ... mo ... something ...* She tried saying the word in her mind. A yawn escaped and another wave of contentment rolled through her body. Making love made her feel so relaxed and in these moments afterwards, safe and cherished.

Chapter Fourteen

lex could hear whispers and muffled laughter. The lush body of Grace that had warmed him all night was no longer pressed against him; he assumed the trio of lassies had pried her away. The furs shifted as something moved towards him. *Grace must be leaning in to kiss me before she goes.* He lifted his forearm from across his eyes and felt a smile spread across his face as he anticipated her sweetness. But, the sweetness that greeted him was warm, wet, and sloppy. Hearing panting and a little whine, he opened his eyes and came face to face with the wee pup Boudica, her soulful eyes desperately pleading for his attention and praise as the women laughed. Wiping the slobber off his mouth, Alex let out a Gaelic cuss that offended all ears but Grace's, with her limited Gaelic. He saw that she was already dressed for the day in a simple kirtle, but ravishing all the same.

"Och, Alex, nae in front of wee Jennet!" Izzy admonished him. "And dinnae rise from the bed, as I ken ye are as bare as the day ye were born," she continued, wagging a finger at him.

Sighing, he placed his arms behind his head and looked to the ceiling. Boudica took this as an invitation to come and lie upon his chest. "Izzy – my dear, sweet, prickly Izzy – I worry to think what ye will come to be like in yer old age."

"That is an easy answer. Pricklier," she said with an entertained snort. "And if my eyes roll back one time too many, they will stay there."

The women turned to leave, except for Grace who came over to him. Smiling, he turned to her. "I dinnae ken whether Izzy will be good or bad company if ye pick up her spitfire ways."

"I will say it is a good thing, if it helps keep you in check." Her voice lowered to a whisper as she walked over to pick up Boudica. "My Highland Heartbreaker," she said softly, pressing a soft kiss to his cheek.

"Where are ye off to today?" he called after her, feeling like a calf-eyed lad as she walked to the door.

"Izzy is taking me on a tour of the keep and the grounds."

"Just ye women alone?"

Izzy, still in hearing distance, shouted back at him. "Ye men! And nay – my *tolla-thon* husband insists a guard accompany us, 'just in case'."

"I am happy with that, then. Off ye all go." Smiling at Grace, his expression softened. "Ye have a lovely day with yer lasses."

After they left, he savoured a few moments of silence. Once he emerged from the sanctuary of the bedchamber, the hustle and bustle of the keep would allow for no moments such as these. He caught sight of his sword that was laid over one of his saddle bags, and he remembered the oddity that he had found last night when he and Grace had retired for bed. He knew Morag said she would leave some type of gift, but how she got it into his chambers at all, let alone so soon after the feast, was beyond him.

He walked over to inspect the object he had found waiting for him. The item that pricked his finger was a *sgian dubh* that had been laid on white heather, slight and almost feminine in its dainty design, and he knew this must be for Grace. Running his thumb over the slim hilt's intricate lines, he observed runes and a Celtic shield knot etched in the surface. On the other side of the hilt was agate, pressed and smooth in a bluish grey shade.

She must intend fer this to protect Grace. But, why will I nae be the one to protect her?

Sighing, he stared up to the ceiling and tried to calm his thoughts which were now shooting in different directions, trying to understand what everything meant. He thought of Morag's riddles, the circumspect fable of the previous evening, and the gnawing feeling in the pit of his stomach that was growing bigger each day. So wrapped in his own thoughts, he did not hear the chamber door open.

"Och, Alex, what makes ye think I wanna see yer arse first thing?" said Jamie, with an exaggerated gag.

"Ye verra well ken this arse of mine is more braw than most men's faces," Alex threw back, happy to break his inner turmoil for some banter.

Jamie rolled his eyes. "Marriage is yet to teach ye humility, it seems, but I verra much look forward to the day yer old and grey with a saggy arse."

"Come now, do ye think that with my smartarse mouth I will live that long?"

Jamie now grinned as he sat on the bed and waited for Alex to find his braies and put a leine on. "What were ye doin', anyway? Ye were absorbed in somethin' when I came in."

Alex had his back turned to Jamie, which gave him the cover-up he needed to speak a little white lie as he pinned his new adornment to his leine. "Nothin' important, except fer knockin' ye flat when we spar today." Alex spun around with a genuine smile. "Ye ken how much I look forward to bestin' ye."

"Aye, I do, and that is because ye are yet to best me," said Jamie, as he stood and made for the door. "In other words, *mo laochan*, soon that bonnie face of yers will be eating dirt."

Boudica napped on Grace's lap while the women took a respite from gardening. Izzy had been teaching her and Kenna more about herbs and flowers and giving offcuts for them to take home and plant. Grace watched Izzy rub her belly and felt a pang of envy, wanting to know how it felt to grow a babe.

"How are you feeling, Izzy?" she asked curiously, not ever having anyone close enough to her to ask. Nanny Bea had never had children of her own.

"I feel fine, more often than not. It is just the discomfort as I grow bigger, and I need to learn to slow down and move differently."

"You seem like such an active person, so I can imagine how difficult it is," Grace replied empathetically.

"I have lots of help, luckily. And when the bairn is born,

I will have Jennet, my ma, my aunt, and Morag; and ye when we visit," Izzy said, smiling warmly.

"Of course! It is really nice we get to spend this time together." Grace watched Kenna and Jennet, skipping and twirling a short distance away.

"Tell me, Grace, while we have these moments alone – how are things, truly?"

Until she started to talk, Grace had no idea how much she needed to unburden her internal dialogue on someone else. Talking to Izzy was different than with Kenna and Nanny, with whom she would not share certain details about Alex, or to Alex and Kenna about the unease their father made her feel. Izzy, close to her age and so open and understanding, allowed her to speak her mind with no restraints and it felt liberating. She told Izzy about Alex's clan still being wary of her, and about the Laird's obvious dislike that had not eased – he was yet to even speak to her conversationally. She shared her surprise – pleasant surprise – at the marriage bed, which led her to sharing her fears about Alex's colourful past. Grace felt relieved when she saw Izzy give an empathetic nod, validating that she was not silly to feel this way.

"I did wonder what led ye to name him the 'Highland Heartbreaker'. To be honest, I am surprised no one thought to name him so before."

"I was aghast at first, that this was the way of the world, but I grew up very sheltered. I did not think women behaved in such a way."

"Aye, it happens high- and low-born, but the high-born will be discreet and the low-born care little. I am what ye would call low-born; my family are farmers and the most wonderful people ye will ever meet. But, my birth parents are high-born – my da is a laird, and my ma died giving birth to me. I dinnae regret growing up the way I did, nae being pampered in the castle. If anything, I imagine it would have been verra lonely."

Grace replied, "That was my life, except for Nanny, but she is like a mother to me more than a friend. The wedding alliance with Alex turned out to be very much a blessing in disguise, despite my initial fears. The prospect of him did frighten me less than my first betrothal, though." An involuntary shiver coursed through Grace's body, causing Boudica to stir and let out a little yip. Grace rubbed the sweet pup between the ears.

"What was frightenin' aboot him?" Izzy's tone was full of concern.

"His name was Gilbert Percy. He was a family friend who came into his baronage early and my father acted as mentor. He was a few years older than me and there was always a sinister shadow about him. He would tell me of animals he tortured, and the first men he killed. He would do so during a meal, whispering in my ear, then laughing as I would scurry away into the waiting arms of Nanny in my chambers. My father cared nought, and once he saw I was coming into my womanhood he simply told me I was now of use, and I was to marry the Baron Percy. From there, I tried to keep all distance from Gilbert, ensuring I was never alone with him. He held such little regard for animals and people, and I knew I would not be any different. He would probably treat me worse than his chattel. He only managed to corner me once and, in that moment, the cold glint in his eye told me all I needed to know. I am ashamed to say that when I heard he had died in a skirmish, I breathed a sigh of relief."

This was the longest speech Grace had ever made, and a noticeable weight lifted from her shoulders, and a ball of nerves that seemed to have sat dormant deep inside her loosened. This unburdening of her soul, while cathartic, tired her and she stifled a yawn.

Izzy came to sit beside her and embraced her. "Never be ashamed. If anyone needed a good killing, he sounds it. And Grace, this has made me really understand part of the cause of yer nerves. Ye have kept a lot of fear inside ye fer a verra long time. And now ye have found safety and friendship. Ye are finding yer inner strength."

"Thank you, Izzy. It does very much feel that way. The advice you gave me also helped a lot – brewing a tea and even a bath have proved very relaxing, both for my mind and body." Grace's face heated as she recalled the bath she shared last evening with Alex. "And I've been feeling safer, Alex's frivolous past aside. I am rational enough to know the past cannot be changed, but I truly hope those ways are behind him."

"Trust me, a little jealousy is nae all bad. It has happened with me, and Jamie, but we both ken we would never want anyone but each other. And I can assure ye, the way Alex looks at ye, I have never seen an expression like that on his face before. He is rapt, and I doubt he is fully aware of it himself yet, since the feeling would be so foreign," Izzy giggled. "But I am so verra glad it has finally bitten him, the bite of love – and bitten him good!"

"Actually, Izzy, you just reminded me of something. Alex said something to me last night in Gaelic." Grace attempted to repeat what he had said and imitated a brogue as she rolled her tongue on the words, "*Mo ghradh.*"

The response from Izzy was a loud squeal accompanied by hand-clapping. A startled Boudica awoke, rolled off Grace's lap, and gave a bark. "He called ye 'my love', Grace! 'My love'!"

"He did? Oh my goodness! I have been seeing little glimpses that he was coming to feel this way, but I did not want to fool myself." Grace felt her face stretch with her big smile as she swept Boudica up into her arms to hug her.

"I am so verra happy fer ye, Grace, and fer Alex. Ye tamed the beast, the 'Highland Heartbreaker'! No mean feat, but ye did it!"

"Now, I will wait to hear him say the words to me in a language I understand, as I yearn to say those words back to him."

Jamie and Alex were rolling around in the dirt as they grappled, trying to get the upper hand to pin the other one down. The men stood in a circle and cheered them on raucously. Alex and Jamie had been wrestling with each other since they were wee lads. They had their moves down to a fine art, as if they were putting on a performance. Nevertheless, they worked up a sweat and aimed to give each other some ache as a reward for their efforts. Alex really needed the physical distraction from his overactive mind and placed all his energy and focus into the movement of his body. The smell of dirt, sweat, and Highland air soothed his soul, and he relished the moment he was being granted. His wayward thoughts relaxed his stance,however, allowing Jamie to obtain the upper hand as he found himself face down in the dirt, Jamie's knee in his back and his arm pulled up back behind him.

"Och, ye bluidy bastard," he groaned, half laughing.

"Aye, tell me ye yield! Yer face is nae as bonnie while ye

eat dirt," Jamie said with satisfaction. Besting each other was a favourite pastime.

"Ye two are worse than wee lads," came Izzy's dulcet tones, and Alex turned his head further to see her. Grace stood beside her, amused.

Jamie let go of Alex's arm and sat back with a contrite shrug. "Lads will be lads, *leannan.*"

"Aye, well ye are both filthy. Go wash up in the loch. We have only a few days left with Grace, Alex, and Kenna, and we must make every moment of it," Izzy informed them. Grace followed with an 'aye'.

"Grace, my bonnie Grace – what say ye come wash my back fer me?" Alex asked her with a wiggle of his brow, drawing a groan from Izzy and Kenna. Grace flushed and he spied her shyness, but also an impish smile at his blatant flirting. He waited for her reply as he saw her thinking.

"I will have to say no, but can I offer you a suggestion?" she teased, somewhat saucily, and he was pleased with her banter.

"And what would that be?"

"To ask Jamie. He got you all dirty, and I know his hands will be less soft, but that will only allow you to appreciate mine more."

Grace turned and walked away, followed by the giggly lasses, and Alex admired the sway of her hips and lush behind.

Grace, Grace, mo ghradh, mo chridhe, ye are making me a verra happy man.

Chapter Fifteen

Alex awoke a sennight later, thinking of the journey they were about to make home, and felt saddened. Before he knew it, they were standing outside in the bailey preparing to take their leave. Their time spent with the Murrays during the day was enjoyable and the evenings spent with Grace heady and sinful. He smiled to himself as he stared at the contrast of her angelic face. He had no more encounters with, nor gifts from Morag. He had not yet given the *sgian dubh* to Grace, undecided on not only how to give it to her, but worried it may spark events he was not ready to face. He was doing a good job of ignoring the sinking feeling that something bad would happen and had just enjoyed every moment of her presence. The scent of lavender constantly permeated the air surrounding her and the slightest inhalation of the scent warmed the space where his heart was. His body and senses were becoming so attuned to her that he felt himself becoming lost within her more and more each and every day.

"We shall be home in time fer Beltane; we will have

much to do," he overheard Kenna telling Grace and Izzy as they shared their goodbyes.

Latha Bealltainn, or Beltane, was the festival that occurs as the Spring Equinox comes to an end and the Summer Solstice begins. It was a time for fires, flowers, feasting, and family. It normally meant much ale and many lasses for him once the work was done. But, this season would be different. He had Grace by his side and he felt a soft smile spread across his lips. He touched the *sgian dubh*, which he wore strapped to his forearm under his leine, and realised this could be the special gift to give her.

"Are ye ready fer the journey home, Alex?" asked Jamie, who came to stand beside him, putting his hand upon his shoulder.

"Aye, and the weather, just like during our time travelling here, holds fast with no brash cold, rain, or winds," he observed.

"It is verra nice. I will nae leave the keep fer some time now. Soon, Izzy will be too round in the belly, then the babe will come and I willnae want to travel too quickly. So, ye will need to take carriage of all the visits over the next few months."

"Dinnae fash, I will. And look at our lassies, thick as thieves. We willnae be able to keep them apart, lest they turn on us," Alex said in a sardonic slow drawl, his comment making Jamie laugh.

The two men joined the women, and they all made their last farewells, embraces, and well-wishes. Jamie helped Grace mount behind Alex, Boudica placed in his lap. Alex saw Grace's soft lily-white hands reach out and pat the pup, who licked her hands, and he felt the vibration of her giggles against his back. He turned the horse and headed out from Aberscross and gave orders to ride at a quick pace, eager to get home. He knew it would be a torturous ride home, stimulating every sensual nerve in his body, and he sighed.

"If ye need or want to stop, Grace, just tell me," he told her over his shoulder.

"I shall. I do think I am becoming more familiar and feel quite safe on horseback now."

"Enough so that ye are willin' to try to learn?"

"Perhaps ... I do find myself feeling braver."

"Aye, ye are. Us Scots have been a good influence on ye."

"I do feel at home with you and Kenna, and the Murrays, more so than I ever did back home in England."

He heard no sadness in her voice as she said this. Acceptance, strength, and pride clutched at his chest. Feeling pride for another was an uncommon feeling, but he let go of a rein to squeeze her hand. They had ridden outside Murray lands and were riding along a path lined by a thicket of trees, and his warrior instincts began to prickle and he instinctively tensed.

"What is it, Alex?" whispered Grace, as she felt the change in his posture. Even wee Boudica who was curled up in a basket on Alex's lap began to growl. He scanned the trees and whistled to his men, a specific tune to alert them. He felt as if they were being watched, but he saw and heard nothing. He sensed Grace's panic growing, as she fed off his own alarm, and tried to calm himself. The feeling of eyes on him gave him a sense of danger, but it did not feel immediate; it was more sinister, like someone held malice towards them. He knew everyone was awaiting his instructions, but he did not know how to explain what he was sensing. He turned to look at Grace and saw her widened eyes.

"It is alright, *leannan*, I willnae let anything or anyone hurt ye."

"Why do I sense your uneasiness, Alex? It was palpable a few moments ago," she said breathily, and he realised she still squeezed his hand tightly in concern. He squeezed it back in comfort.

"'Tis alright, Grace, I dinnae mean to frighten ye. I am just cautious out in the open."

He felt her start to relax and she gave him a faint nod to indicate she was okay. He lifted his other hand and gave everyone a reassuring smile, ignoring the menacing presence, as while he knew it meant harm, it did not mean harm today.

Hagalaz – patience and protection.

"All is well. Let us carry on towards our lands."

Balla Cloiche was bustling, more so than Grace had seen in her short time in residence. And of most import, everyone was in a joyous mood! Grace marvelled at the changes that had happened in the few weeks they had been home. The clan were usually in good spirits, but with more of an air just contentedly getting on with their days. Grace was learning how meaningful, if somewhat superstitious, the Beltane celebration was to the Scots. Grace, Kenna, and Nanny had been working hard as any of the clan women, cleaning the keep while the men gathered the wood. Hunting and gathering had been shared by all, and the kitchens had been cooking for the feasts nonstop in preparation for all hearths and fires being put out.

The smell of meat succulently roasting had Boudica

salivating at her feet, but it was becoming good practice for Grace to teach her 'sit' and 'down'. Boudica was already growing large in the few short weeks since they had returned, and was dedicated to Grace, as Grace was to her. Alex had given her some riding lessons and she had now mastered a slight trot while Alex and Boudica urged her on. Alex had become decidedly protective, insisting Grace always have him or Boudica at her side, and instructing her to never wander far from Kenna or his men. She had taken to rolling her eyes at him, a habit she had picked up from Izzy, which in turn made Alex groan. He would not share the cause of his paranoia (Nanny told her it was a sign of love), so Grace decided to humour him. And when he was not being overprotective, he was setting her aflame with his insatiable lust, and her own now rivalled his. The passion and tenderness was a beautiful thing to experience.

Not that she wanted to admit this thought out loud. Finding her inner strength of late, she did still revel in being cared for so, even if he was yet to tell her that he did love her. Inner strength or not, she still lacked courage as his heartbreaker past still caused a pang of alarm whenever she saw how the women in the clan openly ogled him. Still, she hoped he would find some peace and not stress. Even his father no longer presented as an issue, as he never seemed to be around, and when she did catch any glimpse of him, he seemed to look straight through her with no emotion. Whilst not an ideal relationship, she preferred that to his blatant disdain.

This is where Nanny and Kenna found her, in the Great Hall, deep in thought and chewing on a stalk of wheat. Beltane was at last upon them this day, and Grace wanted everything to go especially perfect.

"Are you okay, Grace? You look as if you are doing some

very serious wool-gathering. Shall I make you some of your calming tea?" Nanny asked, her brow furrowed.

Grace placed down the flower crown she was making and shook her head. "Just lost in thoughts, Nanny. Not bad ones, though. My nerves have been well of late."

"That they have, and I could not be more glad for it. What a change people and environment make, aye?"

"Nanny! You are starting to sound like a Scot!" Grace replied with a laugh. The 'aye' had definitely come out with a lilt.

"Grace, if ye are finished with the crowns, let us get dressed," said Kenna eagerly.

They had found white cloth and lace and fashioned up two of Kenna's plain kirtles with delicate fabric, as well as fresh and dried flowers.

"Let me check on the cake and I will meet you in your room," Grace said with a smile as she stood and smoothed her kirtle. Mrs Cook had shared with her that at every Beltane, they made what was called *am bonnach brea-tine*, and it was a favourite of Alex's. Mrs Cook was fiercely protective of her recipe but had agreed to let Grace help on the basis that she would not press for the secret spices that made it special. There were many eggs to crack, and she had watched on in fascination as Mrs Cook scalloped the edges, the cake growing larger and larger. Mrs Cook had given her a brief overview of the evolution of the Beltane traditions in the Highlands. Growing up along the border, Grace had heard stories of sacrifices during this holiday, which Mrs Cook waved off as ancient pagan doings.

"Aye, there is much mystery and witchery, but nary a sacrifice to be seen, unless ye count the extra beasties ready to be supped upon. Beltane fer us MacNichols is a simple and old-fashioned time to celebrate the change of season and bring forth the cleansing fire fer prosperity and fertility. Ye watch how many bairns the clan is blessed with in the months to come," Mrs Cook informed her with a knowing nod. "Mayhaps a wee future laird."

Grace recalled how the young lasses assisting had giggled and whispered of trysts the night would bring. Between that and Mrs Cook's predictions, she felt her face heathen in a blush. "Mayhaps, Mrs Cook. I do thank you for all your help and knowledge you have been sharing with me. It truly makes me feel like I belong."

Finishing her inspection of the cake, enjoying the spicy aroma that tantalised her taste buds, a wry thought popped into her head: *Another favourite part of the holiday for my husband, I assume – the uninhibited morals of the evening that the Highland Heartbreaker no doubt revelled in.*

Alex had already made his way to the north of the keep, Kenna promising to bring Grace as soon as they were ready. Unbeknownst to them both was Aran, who waited to keep an eye on them. Alex observed the finishing touches to the bonfire and fingered the *sgian dubh* he had strapped to his waist under his leine. This was his first holiday with Grace – *Latha Bealltainn*. It had always been a favourite time, the flames and smoke evoking daring and passion. A celebration of light and purification. Blessings for fertility of the animals and the land, and of course the people. Alex smiled wryly at the thought, as the Beltane fire usually led to an amorous evening as well.

This year would be different, and he had no regrets. When he awoke before Grace, he found himself watching her in contentment. The unease he could not shake disappeared in these moments when he knew she was safe by his side. He was yet to find the words to express how he felt. He was also looking for words to praise her bravery. He was looking forward to gifting her with a weapon of protection.

He heard his dad's voice and looked up to see he was headed in his direction, towards the bonfire to commence the festivities. Much of the clan had already gathered, so it was almost time. He ensured his expression was nonplussed and greeted his father with a laconic *'feasgar math.'* He got a nod in return. They stood there in silence for a few moments until he saw his dad spit on the ground. *Och, he is charming.*

"What is on yer mind, Da?"

"I was thinkin'."

Silence again. Alex held back a sigh. "Aye, and what were ye thinkin'?"

Instead of responding to him, Ewan turned to the clan around them. "MacNichols, my clansmen and clanswomen! *Latha Bealltainn* has come to grace us. This year, we celebrate anew, different from other years. My son, Alex, yer future Laird, now has a wife of his own and with the lighting of this fire tonight, I hope he is soon blessed with a son of his own!" The last few words were drowned by a raucous roar from the clan.

They whooped and whistled, and he spoke again when they quieted down back to a low hum. "And with that said, I give the right to light the Beltane fire to my son, and may he be blessed always."

Alex watched his dad walk over and pick up the branch put aside to light the fire and turn back to walk towards him. Alex wondered with suspicion at the sudden change in his behaviour and supposed acceptance of his marriage. He also wondered why his father was handing this rite – the tradition he so enjoyed of being the one to light the fire – to him, the son who had always disappointed him.

Alex heard murmurs and looked around to find the source of the ado, and his eyes settled upon Grace. His breath hitched in his throat as he felt his heart literally skip a beat at the vision she portrayed. She was draped in white, and rather than wash her out, it made her glow mystically in the dark night, her hair worn long and spread around her like a halo. Aye, mystic and bewitching, like a Celtic sorceress. She gave him one of her sweet smiles and he walked towards her with his arms outstretched, and for a moment everything surrounding them drifted away as her palm met his. He turned to the clan with a sense of pride, the branch to light the fire in his right hand and her hand in his left.

"Aye, I am blessed; a vision of all that is good by my side, a fine night to welcome in Beltane, and to bless our clan, one and all, fer a prosperous and fertile year!" He said the last two words with an exaggerated wink that drew more cacophony from the clan. He drew Grace closer and dipped her in a quick, hot kiss and smiled against her lips as he heard the whistling and the heat from her flushed face. He let her go to kindle the start of the fire, lighting first his branch, then the bonfire. Within seconds it was aflame and there was silence as the beholden sight was revered. One by one, people came forward to light their own branches, to use the fire at their own hearths to cleanse and bless, while others moved towards the long tables set up with food. Alex spied a few couples already making their way off, hand in hand.

"Are you wishing that was you, Alex?" asked Grace, her tone light and playful.

However, he heard a faint insecurity and immediately

felt a sense of guilt at his libertine. He drew her into his arms and nuzzled her neck, inhaling her soft floral scent. "Och, Grace, I ken my past is nae perfect, rather like a 'Highland Heartbreaker' as ye have dubbed me, but I promise ye – there is no one else I would rather be with."

This was as far as he could go at this moment, words of love being so foreign to him, that he almost felt shy. Shaking it off, he pulled back to look down at her face and raised his hand to cradle her jaw. She looked up towards him, trusting and submissive, and that alone aroused him. It was as if she read his mind. Or maybe it was because she could feel him starting to press against her, and a soft smile – the perfect balance of innocence and coyness – spread across her face.

"I need ye now, Grace. I need to be inside ye. Now."

Chapter Sixteen

Grace giggled wildly as Alex guided her through a darkened patch of growth and trees. They were still in the vicinity of the keep and MacNichol lands, but at a distance now where it could be just the two of them alone in faraway woods that imps and faeries could call home. The air was heady and smoky. She knew his intent was to make love to her, here outdoors, and as scandalous as it was it only led her to excitement. She felt herself tingle and moisten between her legs, in anticipation of what was to come. He suddenly stopped under a Scots pine, as she had come to learn was the name of the majestic conifer she saw so much of in the Highlands. The glow of the moon shone down between the gaps in the canopy of leaves above. It was enough light for her to see the raw and unbidden lust on his face, the urgency to make her his, and the dominating presence he exuded sent a thrill down her spine. He took a few steps back from her.

"Take off yer dress," he said in a low seductive voice, the command evident.

She obeyed without objection and slipped the sleeves of

her kirtle down her shoulders, pulling it down at the waist until it pooled at her feet. She had a shift on and the material was sheer. She watched his eyes gaze over her from head to toe and she trembled.

"Mmmm, now come here, Grace," he beckoned, crooking his finger at her.

Again, she obeyed silently. Her breaths were heavy, almost a pant as she drew closer to him. She sensed a change in him tonight; she felt his possession of her, his primal need for her. He grabbed her face again, more roughly than he had earlier, and kissed her deeply. He swept his tongue fervently into her mouth without any mercy and she gripped his shoulders to steady herself from the dizzying assault of his lust. He released her lips and peppered hot wet kisses along her neck, and the ferociousness of lovemaking had indeed left her panting for breath. His kisses reached her breasts and he made no move to rid her of her shift. Her hardened nipples strained against the sheer fabric, and he encapsulated one in his mouth. The sensation of him sucking her nipples through the thin material was causing such pleasure that she heard herself moaning loudly against the quiet of the woods as he ravished her breasts.

"Oh, Alex, I cannot bear it," she managed to plead, but all that did was make him ravish her more fervently.

"Ye will bear it. Ye will take all that I give ye. Yer mine," he said with a growl.

His possessiveness heightened her lust, and she clutched his head to her breasts. His kisses started to make their way up to her lips, recapturing them fiercely before letting her go suddenly. For a brief moment, they both stood in front of each other staring, their chests heaving, and Grace was unable to tear her eyes away from the enthralled look she could see in his own. His broad chest glistened with a sheen of sweat, the moonlight flattering his tanned, smooth skin.

"Grace, I want ye to turn around and place the palms of yer hands against the tree," he ordered, and she did as he said.

She felt him yank her hips roughly against him, so she was bent, her bottom sticking out. He traced his hands over her rounded cheeks, gently and with purpose, like he was trying to memorise the curves, the shape. It was so tantalising and the pulsing between her legs was driving her to a desperate need of release. His movements roughened as he drew her bottom to him, and she felt the hardened proof of his own need against her. The position was something new and was almost animalistic, but that only made the moment more erotic as her breathing faltered in anticipation. His hand slipped between her legs, and he groaned in satisfaction.

"Ye are such a good lass, Grace, *mo chridhe*. Yer want fer me is almost as much as my need fer ye. I cannae help it, how badly I need ye, all the time. Ye will always be mine."

He bent her further and angled her hips and she felt him enter her from behind, his rough actions belying his gentle words as he plunged himself hard and deep inside her. This position was a new experience of pleasurable sensations and before long, her heavy breaths had become lusty gasps as the tremors of her release wracked her body in exquisite spasms that left her languid and satisfied. Alex had not yet slowed his pace and the primal sounds emitting from him meant he was close to joining her in his own release. But suddenly, she felt the sting of his hand against the flesh of her cheeks.

"Again, Grace. Again, *mo chridhe* – release yer passion," he urged, his words more ragged with each breath.

The slap against her bottom spurred her excitement once more, and she found herself teetering on the edge of another mind-blowing burst of ecstasy exploding throughout her body. They cried out in unison and if it wasn't for the strength of him holding her, she would have fallen to the ground, a puddle of spent lust. The air was filled with their heavy breathing as they tried to steady themselves. Tonight felt surreal, somewhat primal, with how uninhibited they had been with one another. She had stepped outside of her comfort zone of the passion she had come to know, and it only reached new heights for her and left her feeling giddy.

"Are ye alright, Grace?" Alex asked, his voice and face concerned as he used his fingers to lift her face to his.

"I am perfect, Alex, just perfect," she whispered, pressing a kiss to his fingers. She watched his lips turn into a sensual smile.

"'Tis quite the experience we had ourselves. Ye drive my passion to new heights every time I get the honour of touching yer body."

"It is not just my body you touch, Alex – you touch my soul," she said, feeling brave on this magical night of Beltane.

"Aye, as ye do mine, Grace. *Mo chridhe*." She would have to confirm the meaning of this Gaelic endearment with Izzy or Kenna, but even without being certain of the meaning, she knew it conveyed so much depth.

"I actually have a present fer ye," he said, rolling up the sleeve of his leine. "And 'tis the perfect evening to give it to ye."

Grace saw strapped to his arm a small, sheathed dagger that he removed from his muscled bicep.

"It is a *sgian dubh*, a small dagger fer ye to hide on yer person, in case ye ever have need of it," Alex explained, as he handed her the weapon.

The dagger was light, but she felt its power all the same. Silver and slim, she ran her finger over the etchings on the hilt and felt Alex's gaze firmly fixed on her.

"Ancient and protective carvings, Grace. Dinnae be fooled – the *sgian dubh* willnae stop ye from getting into trouble; but if ye find yerself in trouble, it is there to help, and to provide ye with protection."

"Where do I keep it? How will I use it?" she asked curiously, feeling a slight surge of power shift through her as she fingered the blade.

"Lemme tie it to yer thigh. Push yer skirts aside. And dinnae fash, my eager lassie – I will teach ye," he said flirtatiously, charming her with one of his sexy grins.

With no hesitation she lifted her kirtle, exposing her ankle, then her calf, until the fabric rested above her knee and she saw his eyes darken in desire. She blushed at her own forthrightness, but held his eyes.

"I am ready for any lessons you want to teach me right now, Alex."

Alex faced his father over the table a few weeks after Beltane, his mind drifting away as it often did to that impassioned night in the woods. He had been so busy since that evening, he had spent little time with Grace, even during the nights. Sometimes, he was too tired or she was already deep in slumber. The times he did have with her were briefly after they broke their fasts in the mornings, when he would take her through learning how to use the *sgian dubh*. He was surprised at how quickly she took to the small weapon. Her movements were swift and sure, which made up for the lack of weight behind it. He made her a makeshift dummy kept in the far gardens, since no one but Grace and Kenna spent any time there, and he implored her to practise every day. While she did give him the adorable roll of her eyes, she humoured him and did practise.

Otherwise, it was not that unusual to be busy with the clan duties after Beltane. He always had been hands-on with the people, helping them plough the fields, and hunting and gathering food. But, he had now taken it upon himself to use this time to tighten security on their lands. There was extra training, and shifts of men patrolling their surrounds. Fortifications of the keep were also underway. There was nary a pair of hands idle in the clan; everyone was working. The Laird himself, still in poor humour, ignored the sight of Grace, which Alex had decided was better than throwing filthy looks her way. But, Alex could not rid himself of the foreboding feelings that still lurked. He turned his attention back to his father, who was updating him on the fortification of the stone wall east of the keep.

"Are ye worried we may be attacked, or has there been some threat?" his dad queried.

"Nay, 'tis all precautionary."

"Aye, I dinnae disagree, but I cannae help but wonder why. It seems we are doing things usually spread across months, all at the same time."

Alex shrugged, not wanting to entertain the suspicious tone.

"I am Laird. Dinnae shrug yer shoulders at me, even if ye are the future Laird."

"Da, I am just wary of any threat. Scotland is still nae at peace, with each other or the land beyond," Alex said, purposely not mentioning England.

His dad spat on the ground. "Do ye nae feel ready fer any fight we may find ourselves in?"

"Nay, that is nae my meaning. I ken our clan's abilities; a fight doesnae worry me, and a wee skirmish would be welcomed fer a bit of fun." The men at the table cheered and pounded their mugs of *uisge beatha* against the table, drawing a wry smile from his dad. "But, a smart warrior still likes to have the measure of any impending outside threats."

"Fair point, but trust me when I say dinnae fash, son – there is nothin' fer ye to worry aboot. I have everything inside and outside the clan under control."

Even though he still spoke in an even tone, Alex felt the skin on his neck prickle and his eyes narrowed. His dad noticed and smiled at him.

"Aye, my son. Dinnae fash."

Alex stormed away from the meeting, Aran in tow, and headed towards the training grounds. He needed to work off some frustrations before retiring for the evening. He and Aran had a sparring routine and mock sword battle down to an art, spirited enough to leave them winded but without any serious injuries. When they were finished, Aran placed a hand on Alex's shoulder and he turned to meet his eye.

"Ye are nae yerself, Alex. Unburden yerself, *mo laochan*," Aran said.

Alex welcomed this moment more than he realised he had needed it. He didn't even feel awkward to have Aran's hand on his shoulder, comforting him like he was a wee lad. Now, he needed to find the words to explain something he could not see or touch, just feel. He took a deep breath and shook his head to clear it and try to gain some clarity.

"I will try and explain to ye, but 'tis hard, as 'tis just a feeling. A sense of foreboding deep in my gut, like something bad is aboot to befall us." Alex searched Aran's eyes for any indication that he understood; but all he saw was confusion mixed with pity, and he sighed despondently. "I cannae make sense of it. I sound daft, aye?"

Aran shook his head. "Nay, Alex. I confess I dinnae understand or have any answers fer ye, but yer instincts are to be trusted and I have never doubted ye. Trouble is brewin' from the sounds of it, whether it be near or far, and ye are being warned," Aran told him solemnly.

This led Alex to think of Morag and her predictions and warnings of the runes. He hoped it would not curse his luck to speak out loud of it. *Berhana* – family, life, and loss.

"Aye, Morag, the *seann bhuidseach* of the Murrays, warned me of danger she saw in the runes. A danger that follows me and Grace. When I am away from her, the feeling grows strong, but when I am with her and ken she is safe in my presence, it eases. And I am sorry to say this, but this feeling worsens more when I am around my da."

"Ye ken yer da is my Laird and I am loyal to the clan, so dinnae be offended when I speak of this," said Aran, and Alex gave him a reassuring nod. "But, there is something changed in him. There is a bitter streak that makes him nae of sound mind at times, and I pray this feelin' ye have is nothin' to do with him."

Alex felt Aran's scrutiny looking for any kind of offence,

but Alex slowly nodded in agreement. In the distance he heard a howling, but tried to focus on Aran. "Aye, ye have voiced my own suspicions, I feel guilty to say. Thank ye, *mo laochan.*"

As he said the words, an icy hand of dread clutched at him, and he knew something was wrong as the howling grew louder, and desperate. It was Boudica! His mood shifted to one of panic and fear, and not just his own, but that of Grace. The synchronisation of becoming attuned to one another had become so powerful that he could sense something had happened. Or, was it admitting to his friend that he feared his own father would betray him? Either way, the fear that had clutched at his gut now spread throughout his body.

"Alex, what is wrong? Ye have lost all colour in yer face," Aran said, as his eyes darted around their surroundings, hand hovering over the hilt of the sword above his shoulder.

"Something has happened, Aran — something with Grace! Haste ye back to the keep!"

Alex had already turned and begun running as he spoke. His mind raced as he thought of the last time he had seen her, and how much time had passed for something to have befallen her. He tore up the stone steps of the castle, opening up all the doors and calling her name until Nanny appeared.

"She and Kenna are in the gardens; what is the matter?" Nanny asked with her brow furrowed in concern. He did not respond and made haste to the gardens behind the kitchen. He could hear the whimpers of Boudica and followed the sound, Aran at his heels. The sound took them further away from the gardens and Alex saw a body lying on the ground near a basket that was moving from side to side. His heart thumped wildly as he approached and saw the tear-stained face of his sister, hands tied and mouth gagged, peering up at him. Next to her was Boudica, tied to a tree with a basket on her head, causing the disorientated whimpers. He and Aran made quick work of freeing them and he rubbed his sister's arms to help the blood flow and comfort her as he asked where Grace was.

"Oh, Alex, it was horrible! These men took her! When Boudica lunged, a man went to stab her and Grace ordered Boudica still. They didnae talk much but they were Scots, Alex. When they tied us up, I thought they were to rob us, but they took Grace. She tried to thwart them, and one of the brutes knocked her on the head with the hilt of his sword and threw her over his shoulder," Kenna sobbed.

The sound of her voice faded as blood rushed to his ears, pounding with the force of his rage and fear of what had happened to Grace. Everything that he was before they met did not exist – the laconic fool, the 'Highland Heart-breaker'. Grace was the light of his life, and he would only see darkness till he had her back.

Chapter Seventeen

Grace gained consciousness and instantly felt sensations of discomfort and pain, as her nerves peaked. Her head ached from the blow she'd received, and her stomach jolted painfully and repeatedly as if something was pushing into her, making her nauseated. She tried taking a steadying breath and instead gagged on the stench of stale sweat, and slowly tried to open her eyes. She saw through her lashes dirt and grass and turned her attention next to what she could hear. All was quiet except for the clip-clopping hooves of horses, and she forced herself to open her eyes fully, fighting through the pain as her eyelids opened.

Taking in her surroundings, it became clear that she was on a horse. However, she was not seated; instead, she saw that she lay across a man's lap as she spied his large hairy calf. *Oh, dear god, I have been abducted and laid out like a sack of wheat.* And the sights of Kenna trussed and Boudica being threatened came back to her memory. The realisation of the situation, and being upside down, caused bile to rise in her throat. She quickly closed her eyes again and fought the urge to vomit with a low moan.

"Are ye awake, *Sassenach*?" someone asked in a deep brogue that was cold and had no empathy.

Trying to remain calm and take steadying breaths, Grace considered her options.

Do I attempt to engage this ruffian in some kind of conversation? Do I squeeze my eyes shut and hope this is all one terrible nightmare?

Her inner voice – the one she had been accustomed to all her life, the voice that spoke through her nerves and angst – told her to make herself small, meek, and mild. All the while, her heart beat madly against her chest while the blood rushed to her ears. She knew what it was to be afraid and feel helpless, just like the time the Baron had cornered her, and she held back a sob. She lamented woefully how stupid she was to believe she would ever change. The move to Scotland. Marrying Alex, a stranger, but now her love. Kenna and the Murrays, her chosen family. Finding herself. *I found ... I found ... myself. I FOUND MYSELF.*

A new inner voice roared throughout her, battling against the negative dialogue she had become so attuned to. This new voice was telling her to breathe and stay calm. It reminded her of how far she had come, the lessons learned and the new experiences that had shaped her into a stronger and more confident person. The Grace of old may have fallen to bits, but this Grace was determined to keep her wits. She thought of Izzy, who would be ropable to be in such a position, but she would also be shrewd in strategizing her next steps.

Grace steadied her breathing and when she trusted herself to speak and not sound hysterical, she spoke. "Yes, I am. May I ask where we are headed, my lord?" She hoped her voice portrayed an unconcerned but respectful nonchalance. The man continued on with his lack of respect and utter rudeness as she heard him spit and laugh.

"I ain't no laird, *Sassenach*. But, dinnae fash– ye will soon be with a lord." His strong brogue did not quite pronounce 'lord' in the high-handed manner she assumed he was going for. And what lord could he be referring to? The only lord she knew was her father and she highly doubted he would go to these efforts to get her back.

The stream of logical thinking and questions to herself had calmed her down and her breath was coming to her more naturally, so she ventured another query. "Pray tell, to which lord do we go? And are we still in Scotland, or do we travel to England?"

"None of yer business, but I can tell ye we willnae be crossing over the border of that shite," he sneered, spitting on the ground. "If ye want to get there soundly, stop yer yammerin'." Grace heard the men riding beside him say 'aye' in agreement.

Not to be deterred, she at least needed to be upright, not only to see her surroundings but to ease the discomfort and nauseating feeling of being transported like a sack of grain. "I will be quiet; however, I do need to be upright, if you please. I would not want to be sick either upon you or your horse," she said, admiring the strength she heard in her own voice.

He grunted and halted his horse to a stop, and spoke Gaelic to the men who also stopped. All she had learned so far was nowhere near enough to understand what they spoke of. He got down off the horse and roughly hauled her down to her feet. Her legs, weak and fatigued, shook as she tried to stand, the blood rushing through her extremities as she readjusted to gravity. She heard the men guffaw at her discomfort, and she shook her body in full like Boudica did and straightened herself, subtly feeling around her waist. Her pouch! She still had it. She got a good look at her captor, long-haired and bearded, his gaze holding no sympathy. Without warning, he yanked her towards him.

"Ye want in front or in back?" he asked with a lewd smile.

"I will sit behind you, if you please." It felt odd to be using such impeccable manners in a situation like this, but it only bolstered her sense of calm.

"At least we can speed up the pace now," he grunted.

He let go of her and mounted the horse, and another of the men came over to her and lifted her up behind him. Disgusted as she felt, she placed her arms and hands at his sides and rested the side of her face against his back. She allowed herself to keep her mind blank as they proceeded to ride, before she reassessed her situation. There was only tree after tree; they could be anywhere. And if they were to stay in Scotland, the Highlands and Lowlands were vast.

Her *sgian dubh* was secured and hidden under her kirtle, strapped to her calf. Alex had been teaching her, but she did not have the skill to beat off a group of men. The only option she currently had was to stay alive and wait until they arrived at this mysterious lord (who was clearly English from the way the brute had emphasised 'lord' and not 'laird') and try to make sense of it then. Any attempt at escape now would only result in harm coming to her, or if she succeeded in getting away, being lost in the woods. True to his word, her captor picked up the pace and she closed her eyes to keep from being sick as the scenery blurred beside her. Focusing on her breathing, she could not help but feel that her pouch from Izzy and *sgian dubh* from Alex were giving her hope.

Grace felt the journey had lasted at least three days, though it felt as if it had taken three weeks. Minimal stops. Minimal privacy. Even her ablutions kept her prisoner, but at least her captor looked the other way. She was cold, tired, and dirty, and her mood had started to border on delirium when she spied a derelict keep within her sights. There was not much activity from what she could see; it lacked the hustle and bustle of Balla Cloiche. Her captor rasped something Gaelic to one of his men who sped up to a gallop towards the keep. She closed her eyes and thought of Alex, repeating to herself to remain steadfast. He would come for her; he would find her.

She heard more talk and then the horse she sat upon sped up to a gallop as well. She opened her eyes to watch their descent into what she could only think of as a beast's lair. The stone walls were bleak, and she only saw shades of grey, brown, and black. Stark and muted. Her spine tingled with alertness, and she straightened herself in the seat as it dawned on her she would soon meet the orchestrator behind this debacle. The familiar feelings threatened to overcome the resolve she had worked so hard for. Her vision darkened and her breathing quickened, hitching in her throat as nerves began to cloud her mind.

"What is the matter with ye, ye daft lass?" asked the brute that had come to assist her off the horse. She did not answer and focused on calming her breath.

"I think she is touched. Look at her – she is like a

cornered *madadh-allaidh*, eyes darting and breathin' ragged. All she is missin' is the snarl!" The long-haired one guffawed at what he thought was his own wit. His idiocy started to calm her, as the reality of his insulting comparisons and descriptions set in. She pulled herself free from his grip and stumbled forward, grabbing the bridle to steady herself. Her wobbly steps resulted in more laughter from the men.

"Quiet!" someone commanded in a strong Scottish brogue, and the men ceased laughing immediately.

"Bring the lass to me."

A man yanked her arm forward and she walked to meet a man with orange hair and a beard, unbrushed and tinged with grey.

"Welcome, milady, and I hope ye will forgive the lack of hospitality yer greeted with. I will escort ye to yer room, where my women await ye with a bath and some refreshment. I ken it will have been a difficult journey fer ye."

She followed him with relief at his fair treatment, the first she'd had in days, and ventured a question. "Thank you for your kindness. May I ask that you share with me the purpose of my being brought here?"

"I cannae, miss — I dinnae have all the details myself, ye ken. What I do ken is someone has given me the promise of gold to have ye brought here by my men. Dinnae fash yerself; there is no intent to bring ye harm, English or not."

"Your men did not treat me kindly," she retorted, frustrated with the lack of explanation. "And I am not sure if you are aware of who I am, but I am married to Alexander MacNichol." Pride was notable in her voice as she relayed the last. He smiled at her, though it lacked warmth, and she realised she had found no ally in this man.

"Aye, I gave no order to treat ye well or poor. Just to bring the English lass married to that tit-lovin' fool. Excuse me language, but yer husband is no better than a whore, with all the skirts he has been under." All propriety of his previous attempts to be nice now dropped. "And from what I ken of yer husband, he will be too busy with another lass, so it will be some time before he becomes aware that yer missin'."

Grace stepped back as if she'd been slapped. She knew Alex had a salty reputation – she herself had dubbed him the Highland Heartbreaker – but it hurt to be belittled so by this crude stranger. He now stopped before a chamber door and gave her a laconic bow.

"Yer chamber awaits, milady."

He yelled out in Gaelic and the door opened for him to push her inwards, into the arms of two young women, sallow and sullen. But, as promised there was a bath, positioned in front of a fire, and a fresh kirtle laid out on the bed. Despite their standoffish demeanour, there was comfort in being in the company of women again and she proffered a small smile.

"How do you do? My name is Grace."

They turned to each other then back to her, shaking their heads. *"Chan eil mi a 'bruidhinn ach Gàidhlig,"* one responded.

Grace gave a weak smile. She knew minimal Gaelic and they knew no English. She desperately wanted to feel clean, and to think, and a bath would provide her that solace, even if it was only for a few moments. The women went to help her undress, but she shook her head, and they turned away in understanding. But, it was not privacy she sought, but a moment to remove her *sgian dubh*, and she quickly hid it under the fresh kirtle. She turned to step into the water which was warm and soothing, and a sigh escaped her lips, and in that moment she almost forgot her circumstances.

The fleeting moment passed, and she felt her nervous system rile up again. She closed her eyes and focused on her breath, not wanting the women to see her distress. One of them poured water over her head and began to gently knead clean her scalp. The niceness of the action calmed her. They may be standoffish, but their manner was still kind. The cleaner she started to feel, the cobwebs clouding her mind began to wear away and she opened her eyes.

She gazed around the room and saw the only exit was the door, as what appeared to be a window was boarded. Escape at present seemed futile, and she pondered her options. If she was difficult or hysterical, they would surely keep her locked up. But, perhaps if she pretended to have some kind of cooperative facade, she would find some opportunity. She needed to ensure her *sgian dubh* would be easily accessible if needed. Just the thought of having to use the weapon caused her heartbeat to quicken and she shook her head.

The women stepped back taking it as a sign she was done, and she was handed a drying cloth. She quickly took it and stepped out and moved to the bed, so they did not try and assist with her clothes. They turned their attention to the bath, using buckets for the excess water. She used this time to dry herself hurriedly and dress. The evening seemed to be passing quickly as she sat herself in a chair and the maids went about their business, Grace watching with alertness. She was brought food and drink, and other servants came in and out to remove the bath. She moved back to the fire to brush her hair with the comb they provided and as the last person left and closed the door, she allowed her alertness to drop a little and her shoulders slumped as she breathed out a heavy sigh.

At that moment, the door opened and she turned quickly, startled. The person who stood in the doorway turned the blood in her veins to ice.

Chapter Eighteen

Alex stormed around the keep yelling obscenities and threats that even made his men wince at their vehemence. Kenna's tear-stained face watched him prowling. *Aye*, she thought, *he was doing just that.* Prowling like a lion, powerful and menacing as he roared his despair and rage throughout the keep.

"What is all the hollerin' aboot, Alex? Goddam lad," his dad asked, scowling and annoyed at the commotion.

Alex spun around, his body vibrating with fury. "What is my hollerin' aboot, ye ask? My bluidy wife has been taken, ye old fool! Taken from our verra own keep and yer verra own daughter hurt in the process!" Alex cried, pointing a finger towards Kenna. "And I swear on everything sacred I will find her and make the clan who has done this pay. I will rain hell down upon them."

"Ye would have our clan be drawn into a blood feud over a *Sassenach*?" his father sneered in reply.

"My wife!" Alex roared with such ferocity that Kenna could swear the foundations of the keep trembled as the vibration echoed off the walls. She saw her dad take a menacing step towards Alex whose own eyes held a dark rage, and she quickly ran to step in between them.

"Stop it, both of ye! Let us turn our minds to finding Grace and nae fighting one another!" she cried, facing her dad.

Ewan's face softened as he held a hand up to her bruised face. "I am sorry ye got hurt, daughter."

The regret in his voice was genuine and Kenna gave him a small smile. "Dinnae fash, Da. I will be fine physically, but my heart cannae take ye and Alex fighting with each other. And yer feelings aboot Grace aside, she is Alex's wife and I see her as my sister. We want her back."

"Thank ye, Kenna," Alex said solemnly in a much calmer tone, though she could hear his breathing was still heavy. The silence now in the hall allowed them to hear the sobs of Nanny, who was being comforted by Mrs Cook. Kenna ran over to offer solace, leaving Alex to face his father again.

"I need a calm head and to think of my plan. Ye can either assist me or leave me be. The choice is yers, but I will tell ye one thing: I willnae tolerate any unkind comments aboot Grace." His dad blinked at him for a few moments, as if he had just realised something, but did not speak. Instead, he turned and walked out of the hall.

Something stirred within Alex, that same niggling feeling he kept getting in the pit of his stomach. *Ehawaz* – betrayal. That is what the feeling was. A sense of betrayal, just as Morag had warned. *Mo dhia*, he swore to himself; the events were unravelling before him, but he still could not grasp the sense. The protection she spoke of clearly related to Grace and he felt shame at his inability to do so. She had trusted him. Even after dubbing him the 'Highland Heartbreaker', she had kept her faith in him. He thought of the growth and strength she had found within herself, compared to the wide-eyed panic he had first seen in her eyes. He shook his head and tried to recall the rest of Morag's warning. She said she had sensed familial life or loss, or perhaps both, and he looked in the direction his father had taken and noted the abysmal presence he had left in his wake.

"Alex, are ye alright? I am seeing emotions flicker across yer face and I dinnae ken what to make of it?" Aran asked worriedly, and Alex looked at him.

"It was him, Aran. It was Da. He is entangled in this; the orchestrator of this travesty. Deep down I kenned it, but I wouldnae allow myself to believe it." He spoke the words in a hollow tone. "But, as much as this is his fault, 'tis also mine. I was meant to keep her safe. I had been forewarned by a *seann bhuidseach* and my ... What would ye call it – my pride, my stubbornness? I ignored it all as I didnae want to face the reality that Da was capable of something so terrible. He even allowed Kenna to be injured!" His ire started to gain momentum once again.

Aran placed a steady hand on his shoulder. "Alex, if what ye say is true, and I am verra sorry to say that I think ye are right, ye must keep all wits aboot ye. It is clear that the Laird is nae right in his mind, and I cannae bear to think what he has done. But, fer ye to find out, ye need a plan."

Alex heard the truth and sense of Aran's words, and he forced his breathing to slow down and closed his eyes. He saw Grace in his mind, knew she would be afraid and panicked, and gave himself no option but to focus on finding her. Like in battle, he needed a plan, and the best plans were always laid using clear purpose and strategy, and knowing your opponent's weaknesses. And he knew yelling at his dad, or asking him again if he had done something, would waste valuable time. He needed to approach him directly and simply state he knew it was him and match his ruthlessness. No pleading or compromising.

"Aye, Aran, ye are right." Alex looked over to Kenna and Nanny still huddled and comforting each other, and he walked over to them both. "I am gonna bring her back, trust me," he said quietly, enveloping them both in a bear hug.

"You better, young man," said Nanny when he released them, dabbing at her wet eyes. "Grace had not known much happiness till she came here and met you. This will not be the end of her story. The Highlands are only the beginning," she told him as he held her gaze.

"Aye, Alex, I ken ye will find her. I just hope 'tis soon and nae later; but if anyone can do this, 'tis ye," Kenna told him with sisterly faith shining in her eyes.

He nodded to them both and without words, spun around to go find the Laird of Castle Balla Cloiche.

The pounding of hooves caused a thunderous cacophony across the Highlands. Alex and his men rode the hobby horses, lighter on their feet than the harder and faster destriers. The quick-footed beasts and the heavily muscled Highlanders had ridden with nary a break, desperate to rescue their future Laird's bride. Alex had hoped the stampede of noise would drown out his thoughts of woe, worry, and rage, but it had not eased this burden of the mind. All his mind could see were two scenes that flittered back and forth repeatedly. One was the face of Grace, angelic and trusting as he pictured her in the mornings when he awoke to her in his arms. The other scene was the confrontation with Laird

Ewan. He could not bring himself to call him 'Da'. That he would commit such a torrid, dangerous act, Alex could not even begin to fathom. English or not, she was his wife, and she now bore their name, and was one of their clan.

Alex found him on the parapet looking over their land, hands crossed against his chest.

"Tell me what ye did!" he yelled, his voice tight with fury.

"Do ye really want to hear it, son?" Ewan asked, not even turning around.

"Aye, I want to hear it, and I want ye to turn around and face me like a man." Alex's toneless words reverberated off the stone. He watched his dad turn around slowly and when they came face to face, Alex saw no fight left in his eyes – only defeat and dare he believe it, regret. "Unburden yer soul. Whatever ye did, we can fix it," said Alex, fighting for calm.

"Ye ken how I feel aboot the English, Alex. I thought this was the best thing to do. I didnae want our bloodline tainted with English blood, and I didnae ken yer feelin's fer the lass were so fierce." Ewan searched Alex's face for understanding and Alex managed a curt nod. Ewan continued. "The war has been tough on many clans; nae all fared as well. If ye remember the McCabes, I spent a night in my travels at his keep and shared my ire towards the Bruce, ye, and the English lass. Perchance, he had been caring fer a wounded man, an English man who had sent fer gold and silver to pay him fer his troubles."

Alex started to feel exasperated, wondering where this story was going. "Get to the point. Where is Grace? What did ye do?"

"The man staying at McCabe's keep was that Baron Percy, or Gilbert, some stupid English name. Yer bride's dead fiancé. Except, he is alive, son – and he wants her back. We planned to make it look like a kidnapping, so McCabe's men came and took her. I kenned ye would be mad, but thought ye would move on like ye do with all the lassies. I now fear my hatred has blinded me to what yer true feelings are."

The vision of the regretful expression on his father's face faded from memory, as it was too painful to focus on. He seemed so small and dissolute, and Alex did not want to feel pity. The burning hot rage pumping through his veins did not want that. He wanted his wife. He would deal with the betrayal later. As he rode alongside his men, he focused his mind on the details of the keep and the details of the man who had kidnapped his wife. Scarred and treacherous, alone with Grace. A man he knew she feared, he was cruel and without conscience. At least three days had now passed and the possibility of any terrible thing she had to endure made him cry out in anguish.

"How do ye fare, Alex?" shouted Aran.

"We need to reach her, *mo laochan*. We need to reach her now!" he shouted back, and spurred his horse faster.

Chapter Nineteen

Grace was suspended in shock as she looked at the person standing before her. She shifted between wanting to scream in terror and laugh maniacally. Since she had last had sight of him, his normally pale and unblemished face was now sallow and sported a grotesque scar on his cheek. The skin was an angry red and puckered like it had not been carefully tended to in order to properly heal. He exuded that same malevolence he always had, but it had increased tenfold, and she felt her stomach sour with despair and disgust. Her not so inwardly cringe was not unnoticed, and he smiled. The term 'smile' was almost humorous, however, as the smile held no mirth or goodwill, and the movement caused his face to stretch and made the scar more pronounced.

"You!" she managed to choke out. "But you are dead! How are you the one who has done this? Why?!"

"Why do you think, Grace?" asked the toneless voice of her ex-fiancé, Baron Gilbert Percy. "You should know me well enough to realise I would never allow another man, let alone a filthy Scot, to take what was promised to me."

"I thought ... I thought you were dead?" she managed to repeat as her mind raced wildly.

"Fear not, sweeting, for I am alive, and I am well, despite the disfigurement that saw you recoil in disgust. And by the grace of all things holy, I am alive and well to give you succour from the predicament you find yourself in."

Her body vibrated as she hummed with nerves. Trying to focus on what was transpiring required every ounce of sheer will and she steered her thoughts to Alex.

"Ahh, Grace, my sweeting. Those magnificent blue eyes, still deathly afraid of all life has to offer. Still stuttering and sputtering with every soft word."

His narcissistic insults and insincere compliments would have caused her to cower back home in England, before she had found her true self. She saw his brows lift in surprise as the fire she felt light within her shone in her eyes. She was not the girl he once knew. And he would not shape any part of the woman she had become, and was still becoming. Turning her nerves into strength, she straightened her spine.

"I am *not* your *sweeting*. I am Grace MacNichol, wife of Alexander MacNichol. I cannot even begin to fathom what kind of lunacy brought this about, where you think to kidnap me, but rest assured your nefarious plot will not come to fruition."

For a moment, he stared at her puzzled and she had to refrain from giving him a satisfied smirk – the kind of cocky smile Alex would make with his inexhaustible confidence. But, her feeling of pride lasted only a fleeting moment as he laughed at her. His cackle became a hacking cough and he struggled to breathe, which gave her a little joy back for a moment. Composing himself, Gilbert returned his gaze to her face.

"My, my, the barbaric Scots have had quite the impact on you, Grace. But alas, let us not play these games. Your marriage is a farce. This man you are married to will lift the skirts of any trollop. He is a dimwitted troglodyte. His family will never accept an Englishwoman, a *Sassenach* like you. How do you think you came to be in my possession?"

"How dare you speak of Alex that way? You on your best day could never match him as a man on his worst." The irony that she took such umbrage in hearing Alex described in such a way, when she herself had dubbed him the Highland Heartbreaker, was not lost on her. And for Gilbert to imply that Alex, who had only ever treated her with respect, was brutal in character, when Gilbert was the one who had arranged her kidnapping, was confounding. *The audacity of this despicable beast*, she fumed to herself, as he still watched her with the same sardonic smile.

"You are not listening to me, Grace. A folly of finding your voice, I guess? You are not wanted, and this is how you came to be here. I will take you home with me, we will be married on English soil, and your father will denounce this marriage as a sham."

Her mind raced wildly as she tried to digest what he was implying. Alex would not do this. The clan would not do this to him either, and many had since warmed to her. Where was he getting this from? And why does any of this matter to him?

"Why do you care, Lord Percy, what fate has befallen me? You never held love for me; you barely knew me. I was just a transactional agreement between you and my father."

He nodded in agreement. "Yes, that is right. There was

an agreement, and with that agreement came a docile wife of good breeding and dowry. What is mine is mine, and the only way that anything belonging to me will be taken is if I am truly dead. War is cruel, Grace. You suffer an injury like the one to my face and everyone assumes you are dead and leaves you to rot. My men were cowards. And your father's position was fickle. I will have my revenge on any who cross me."

He paused and eyed her intently, as if seeing her anew, and gave a slight shake of his head. "But, I can see that you are much changed. It is of no matter, however. I will bend you to my will." The menacing tone stopped her from spitting a retort, lest he try now to do so. He turned towards the door, and she still had not asked the other question that had been caught in the back of her throat.

"Please, wait a moment. Pray tell, who is the person that fed you information of my place in the clan?" She hated the desperation in her tone.

He did not even turn around to respond. She just heard his flat, cold voice. "No more questions. I am tired of your presence. I will come see you anon, and you may ask me again then."

What could have only been a few moments later, though it felt an age while she stared at the closed door, one of the women from earlier stepped in. She held a drinking cup to Grace, and she accepted it with a faint smile. She received a nod in return and the woman quickly exited. Grace sniffed the contents of the warmed caudle and the milk at least seemed fresh. She smelt the honey and the faint smell of the *uisge beatha*, 'the water of life' as Alex calls it, and a teardrop rolled down her cheek and dropped into the caudle. She took some chamomile from her pouch, rubbed it into a powder with her fingers, and dropped some in the cup. Moving to sit on the bed and sip at the drink, she allowed the tears to slowly fall down her cheeks.

The situation seemed impossible. She was back in the clutches of a man she abhorred, but she still had this hope deep down that Alex would find her. And in the meantime, she knew she had to keep strong and keep trying to save herself. Seeing Percy, if anything, reminded her of how far she had since come. She could not control the nerves being set upon her, which she could accept. However, she could now control how she reacted when she felt her heart rate increase in discomfort. She had found the use of herbs, but most of all, she had her inner strength.

The caudle had warmed her insides and she got under the surprisingly soft bed linen and laid down on her side, bringing her *sgian dubh* to rest under her hand. The gift provided her comfort as she fingered the smooth, cool metal of the hilt and remembered Alex's words – *hold it tightly, decide on yer target, and take strong aim. Never falter.*

Grace had been sitting for hours, stewing on the events, and she was angry. Not annoyed, nor miffed, but furiously angry to a degree she had not before experienced. Nor did she know such an ire was possible to experience! Cooped up in this room, she had lost all sense of time. The window had been boarded up so she could not see outside. The sounds of the outside world were muffled; was it people whispering, or a bird whistling a morning tune? She was brought food, and water to wash with, but the women spoke no words to her.

The fact that Gilbert had not returned was incensing

her most of all. Her initial horror and panic at seeing him had abated and this newfound anger had taken its place. She did not belong to him – never did and never would. She was Alex's. They were one. Not only in flesh, but heart and soul, and that feeling was giving her strength and fuelling her ire. The everpresent nerves usually urged her to feel danger and run, but the nerves were now telling her to fight. She had kept busy practising with her *sgian dubh*, for if she had to use it, she knew she would only get one shot and needed to use it to her advantage.

She heard the clank of the door unlocking and quickly slid her *sgian dubh* up her sleeve, tied around her forearm. It was one of the women with a tray of bread and cheese. Grace wished she had the spirit to knock senseless this woman and attempt escape, but she would not lower herself to do that. This woman looked like she had lived a life ruled by a man. Whilst this woman was kept in servitude, Grace understood this is the life that could have awaited her if her marriage to Gilbert Percy had taken place. That's how he would have treated her – as a slave, a possession.

As the woman was leaving, Grace heard a man shout in Gaelic. She did not understand the words and heard panic in his tone, but the door shut and locked before she could hear anything else. Hurrying over to the door, she pressed her ear against it and heard yelling and the pounding of feet. The clang of the lock turning again made her jump back in alarm and adrenaline began to rush through her body. She somehow sensed this was her moment.

Gilbert stepped into the room, his face a mask of annoyance as he eyed her up and down with narrowed eyes, causing a shiver to run down her spine. "Maybe your barbarian husband has some feeling after all – pride, perhaps?" he asked snidely.

The feeling of relief that spread through her was so powerful that she had to steady herself. "Alex is here?" *All is not lost.*

Gilbert, seemingly reading her thoughts, sneered. "Yes, but he will not see you. Come, I am going to hide you elsewhere, and myself with you so they think we have gone. His idiot father did not stick to the plan. But, what did I expect in dealing with a Scot?" He yanked roughly at Grace's arm, trying to pull her through the doorway as she resisted with all her weight and might.

Her mind exploded with thoughts as she looked up into his cold, emotionless eyes. *Alex is here to take me home. Gilbert, this despicable creature, was here to take me away.* She was tired of living her life as a damsel, afraid and dependent. With her free arm, she reached into her other sleeve to pull at the hilt of her *sgian dubh*. The quickness of her action took him by surprise, and he stumbled a few steps back as he spied her weapon. She held it in front of her, warning him away.

"Remove yourself from my path. Now! I am not your prisoner. Not now, not ever."

He was still eyeing her *sgian dubh*, but laughed and creeped towards her again. "Do you think a little knife and an unskilled woman will best me?"

Using all her might, she thrust the *sgian dubh* forward just as he stepped toward her, and she felt the sharp steel cut through the flesh of his abdomen. He screamed in shock and agony, but she felt no remorse or panic. She pulled the *sgian dubh* back and he dropped to his knees. She knew the flesh wound, while causing him pain, may only incapacitate him for so long, so she hurriedly stepped over him and ran out the door.

The stone keep was dark and dank. She found a set of

stairs and ran down the spiralled stone, stumbling in her haste and reaching out to the cold walls to steady herself. She found herself in what must be the Great Hall. It lacked the grandeur of Balla Cloiche, but she knew she was closer to escaping out into the open. She could hear men arguing and ran towards the sound of voices, recognising Alex's usual smooth timbre now roaring with anger. She found herself in the outer bailey and the voices became clear. A mix of Gaelic and English was spewing back and forth.

"I want my wife, goddamn ye all! Bluidy bastards! Stop telling me she is nae here. Yer plans are thwarted. Move aside, or I will make ye."

"Alex! Alex, I am here! Alex!" She yelled louder than she ever had in her life, all decorum thrown aside.

"Grace, *mo chridhe*, yer voice is music to my ears. I am coming fer ye!" Alex cried as they caught sight of one another. She saw Alex barge past the men at the gate, his huge bulk bowling over a handful of them as he set his eyes on hers. She had the oddest sensation that the connection of their eyes, and not their feet, was now drawing them closer together. She leapt into his outstretched arms and buried her face in his broad chest as relief made her body feel limp. Alex rubbed his hands through her hair and down her body, firmly rubbing each part.

"Ye are nae hurt. Are ye alright? I am here now, *mo chridhe*, I am here," he murmured repeatedly in hoarse whispers as relief overwhelmed him.

His men had followed suit and barged through and now stood behind them in a protective guard. Tears sprung to Grace's eyes as she realised this nightmare was coming to an end. But, suddenly she felt Alex stiffen in vigilance and she herself sensed a threat coming toward them. She knew it could only be the Baron.

"Where do you think you are going, Grace?" he asked loudly with contempt, but she could hear the undertone of pain in his voice from her attack.

"I am leaving with my husband," she replied just as loudly as she turned around to face him.

"What of my wound, dear heart? You will not stay and tend to the stab wound made by your own hand?" He moved his hand away from his abdomen to reveal the full impact of the damage she had caused and his blood-soaked clothing.

"Aye, I taught my wife well, ye cowardly bastard. She kens how to take care of herself. If ye come any closer, I will be sure to finish off what she started," Alex said menacingly, as he stood in front of Grace to shield her with his body.

"She was betrothed to me. I did not die on the battle-field. I did not rescind my agreement with her father. Your marriage means nothing," he spat out bitterly, sweat pouring down his pale face.

"Aye, it may mean nothing to ye. But, it means every-thing to me – Grace, my clan. She is my wife in name and heart and soul. She is my *còmhla ri anam*, and I love her more than life itself. In my past I was the 'Highland Heart-breaker', and I dinnae deny it." He turned to stare into Grace's eyes with gentle ferocity. "But she is my present and future, always."

Tears sprung to Grace's eyes as he caressed her cheek lovingly. She knew Alex felt deeply for her, but to hear him say these words almost made the torrid events worthwhile.

Alex turned back to the Baron, who glared at them hate-fully. "Ye have two options, Percy. Ye get on a horse and get out of Scotland now, or ye die where ye stand and stay in Scotland till yer bones turn to dust. What will it be?"

For a moment, Grace thought he was about to choose

the latter, but he instead turned and shouted out some orders for someone to tend to his wound.

"With any luck, Grace, that wound ye gave him will be the end of him. That to me will be the perfect justice," said Alex, and he placed a kiss on her nose.

Grace heard a cough and turned to see the Laird of the MacNichol clan looking at her and Alex with guilt and regret, and despite it all, she could not help but pity him. He looked so much older since she had seen him last, and frail. "I, uh ... I wanna tell ye both – and especially ye, Grace – that I am sorry. Verra sorry. My hate made me misguided and I dinnae ken how to make amends. But, I promise ye, there will be no more objections from me."

Alex nodded and gripped her tighter, signifying the impact those words had on him.

"Thank you for saying that," Grace told him. "I want us all to put the past behind us. And I think I can speak for all the MacNichols when I say that it is time to go home." The men all cheered, and Alex swept her up in his arms, his Adonis face beaming at her.

"Aye, let's go home!" he said to his men loudly before turning back to Grace. "*Tha gràdh agam ort*, Grace. I cannae take one more step until ye ken how much I love ye."

Chapter Twenty

The journey home took longer now that Alex was not manic with fear and anger. He needed to ensure Grace got enough rest and nourishment after her nightmarish abduction. They were currently on horseback, and she was curled up in his lap sleeping peacefully and he felt his heart swell with love and pride. He remembered his wide-eyed bride's panic-filled eyes, compared to his brave warrior who had gone from strength to strength since he'd known her. She never had to change who she was, but find the person she had always been deep down.

It was he who had to change and find a better version of himself – someone with depth and purpose. To think he would find it in a soft English lass from the wrong side of the border would have been laughable, but now he owed his contentment to the Bruce himself. Alex grinned to himself at the way it had all turned out. Robert always had a knack of seeing things for more than what they were, which made him not only a good King, but a good friend. And Jamie and

Izzy of course, who would be beside themselves with relief now that Grace was safe.

Aran interrupted his thoughts as he came to report the news of his scout ahead. "The keep is in view, and I can see the Bruce's standards, Alex," he relayed.

"What is it, Alex?" asked Grace as she stirred.

"The keep is in sight, and we have guests. Hold on, *mo chridhe*," he told her as he urged his horse into a gallop. "We are going home."

Alex bounded into the bailey to the cheers of his clanspeople, ecstatic to see Grace astride his horse. Boudica's excited bark rang out loudly over the people as she bounded over to her human. A beaming Robert the Bruce stepped forward to greet them, cheering just as loudly. He came forward to assist Grace down from the horse and swept her into a bear hug, Boudica jumping at his legs.

"Ye dinnae understand how relieved I feel right now to have ye both home and safe, and by all appearances unharmed. I intercepted yer messenger sent to Jamie and made my way here."

"Alex! Alex, yer back. We were ready to come after ye," came the deep brogue from Duncan Murray, who swept him up in his own hug. Jamie's younger brother had grown into his Murray height and bulk in his time away with the Bruce, and Alex hugged him back joyously.

"Look at ye! Ye are a proper Highlander now."

"Aye," said the Bruce. "He is one of my most dependable men, just like ye and Jamie." The Bruce then turned to Laird MacNichol and said, "Unlike some."

Alex knew this was coming and as furious as he was, and it would take him a lifetime to forgive him in full, his dad was still his dad. Before anyone could speak, Grace rushed to his father's side.

"It may not be my place to speak to this, but seeing as I am at the centre of what occurred, I wish to speak." Alex could not help but grin at her spunk, and the Bruce nodded for her to continue. "I want all of us here today to put what has happened behind us. Time will heal the wounds of distrust and betrayal. The Laird is the father of two people I love very much, and I genuinely believe he has seen the error in his ways. He led Alex to me. And the man he plotted with fed into the deep hate many Scots feel for the English. I want to start anew." She held her hands up, palms facing to the sky in a gesture of acceptance.

The Bruce nodded thoughtfully as he considered her words, and looked to the Laird. "And what say ye?"

Laird MacNichol spoke. "Grace, Alex, and ye, my bonnie Kenna. Ye are my blood, and I brought hurt and shame upon ye all. I was blinded by hate and regret my actions. I can see that now, and I wish it didnae take me to hurt my own blood before I could see clearly. But, Alex, and ye Robert, I look at ye both and the wisdom ye wield as leaders of men. That is past me now; I have been an old bitter man fer too long. I wish to step down as Laird and have Alex step into my place and lead the clan. I want to spend my years making amends to the ones I have hurt and serving the clan as a man, nae a leader. I ken ye may banish me, son, and I will nae fight ye if ye do."

Alex was taken aback. The raw humility was something he had never seen in his father. Despite the anger that still bubbled underneath the surface from the destructive path of betrayal he had led them on, it was not in his nature to hold grudges. And if Grace was content to put the events behind them, he could come to terms with it. This was just not what he expected as he looked around at the faces of his father, Grace, Kenna, Duncan, his King, and the rest of the clan who awaited his response. There was a current of energy swirling around him, invisible but present, and it felt like light and new beginnings. He turned back to Grace who gave him a slight nod and an encouraging smile. The forgiveness in her eyes and the calmness of her stance gave him strength.

"Da, I dinnae want ye to leave. Aye, I am furious, and we have many wounds to mend, but that cannae be done if we are apart. I am proud to be Laird of my people, and with Grace as my Lady by my side we will keep clan MacNichol whole and prosperous, protected and sheltered."

Grace ran over to embrace him, and he swept her up in his arms as the clan cheered their approval of his words.

"I am verra grateful to ye both," his dad told them as he walked over. "But, I am gonna take a few days leave to get my head sorted out."

Alex nodded in understanding; it was a wise decision. Ewan MacNichol turned to Grace and gave her a deep bow of respect before walking away.

Grace turned her soulful eyes to Alex. "Alex, look how far we have come together," she said happily, kissing him gently on the lips.

"If ye had asked me before I met ye, if being a married Laird would make me this happy, I would have spat out my ale in laughter. What a fool that man was."

"Beg yer pardon, Alex, milady. I just want to give ye this letter from Jamie," Duncan interrupted.

"'Tis so good to have ye back, Grace. Nanny, Boudica, and I missed ye dreadfully," said Kenna, standing next to Duncan.

Grace hugged Kenna and then Nanny, who squeezed her back fiercely. "Oh, my sweet child, I was so worried about you! It is so good to have you back where you belong." Nanny's voice was thick with emotion.

Yes, thought Grace, as she returned the hug just as fiercely. *This is where I belong.* "Dinnae fash, Nanny, I am well," Grace said cheekily, bringing a smile to Nanny's face with her Scottish lilt.

Grace moved closer to the ground to put her arms around Boudica who was whimpering happily and licking Grace. "It will be a night of celebration for all. Alex and I just need to clean up first."

"I can help ye bathe," offered Kenna, but Alex cut her off, holding up his hand.

"I got that covered, thank ye," Alex grinned, drawing a blush from Kenna and Duncan. A laugh quickly turned into a cough from the Bruce.

"You are incorrigible, Alex," Grace scolded him.

"Aye, he is that," agreed Duncan, who then turned to Kenna with his arm extended. "Can I escort ye to the Great Hall, Kenna? We can catch up."

Alex bit his tongue to stop himself making Duncan and Kenna feel more embarrassed as he watched Kenna eagerly take Duncan's arm.

Grace rose up from the group to whisper into Alex's ear. "How sweet is that, Alex? And what a union that shall be."

"That will be a thought fer another time, *mo chridhe.* All I can think of now is the union of ye and I."

Grace stretched out in the hot scented water as Alex tended to her like a maid. It kept drawing giggles from her, how overly attentive he was being, currently brushing out her hair that he had just lovingly washed.

"Alex, as much as I love you pampering me, I am still waiting for you to ravish me." Emboldened by all that had led them to this moment, Grace leaned back to gaze at him.

"All in good time will I make ye mine," he whispered. His blue eyes glittered seductively as he softly brushed his fingers against her collarbone. "But I want us to talk first." Grace watched the look of confusion cross his face after he said those words and the joy in his smile as he threw his head back and laughed. "Aye, ye bring out the better man in me, *mo chridhe*. I'm thinking with my heart and nae with what's between my legs." His smile faded and his expression grew serious.

Grace noted the fine lines at the corners of his eyes and reached one of her hands up to touch the wisdom newly etched in his skin. "Tell me, what is wrong?"

"I need to ken that ye are alright. 'Tis been an arduous journey and ye have shown the courage of a thousand men, but we havnae spoken aboot what ye endured. And I dinnae want ye to forgive Da and welcome him into our lives if that will cause ye resentment. Ye are nae the same lass that stepped out of that ramshackle cart. Ye are brave and strong; I dinnae want ye to lose that."

His fervent concern brought tears to her eyes. "You are right, Alex. I am a very different lass, and that is why I can put what has happened behind us and look to the future. I do not expect every day to be kind to us and I accept some days my nerves may get the better of me. But, what I do know is with you I am safe, and I am loved, and most importantly I now love myself for who I am, and I will fight to keep myself and those I love safe as well."

Their words spent, he pressed his forehead to hers and

the gesture symbolised their unity in a way different to words. She felt their connection surging between them, soul to soul. There was so much power in this moment and Alex pulled back like he sensed it as well.

"There is one thing I will tell ye. Morag, the *seann bhuidseach* of the Murrays, gave me warnings. She had seen things in the runes, and I regret I did nae heed them. I never believed in magic, but I owe Morag a debt of gratitude. She engraved the *sgian dubh* as well, no doubt protectin' ye."

"We both owe her our thanks. Alex, I just had a thought – you are also not the same man. You never thought to marry and fall in love, with an English lass at that, never thinking you could curb your Highland Heartbreaker ways."

"Aye, verra true. But, I am now a one-woman man, devoted to my bonnie English lassie."

"And now we have settled in our own love, I need someone to tell me more about Duncan Murray! Did you see the way Kenna and he looked at each other?"

Alex groaned. "Aye, I did, and I dinnae even want to think aboot how impossible Izzy and ye are gonna be."

Grace seized the moment. *This is the perfect time to slip in the perfect Gaelic pronunciation I've been practising.*

"Prepare yourself for grey hairs, *mo ghradh – tha gràdh agam ort.*"

Epilogue

Balla Cloiche

Two years later

Alex watched his dark-haired daughter crawl along the furs laid out on the stone floor, determined and sure to reach the large dog sleeping by the fire. He watched on in amusement as she reached Boudica, who opened one eye to see a chubby little finger poking her side. The little cherub squealed with delight, happy to receive the attention, and turned around to crawl back to her dad. Alex was besotted with his wee daughter, Mairi. She had his dark hair but the angelic beauty of her mother, his beloved Grace. Mairi was spirited, brave, and all things that made his heart whole, from the moment Grace learnt she was pregnant. She reached his legs and lifted her arms, demanding he haul her up and he immediately did so, never able to refuse her anything. She rewarded him with a dimpled smile and patted his chest as if to tell him he had done good. He looked up as he heard Grace's footsteps and smiled at her as she came towards them.

"Hello, my loves. What a pretty pair you make," she smiled, leaning over to kiss them each on the forehead.

"What are ye up to this fine morn, *mo ghradh?*"

"I was just checking on the garden, and cutting some blooms. I also intercepted a messenger who had a letter for us from the Murrays."

Mairi was now reaching her arms towards Grace, wanting her mother's attention. Grace happily obliged, placing a kiss on her perfect button nose. Alex knew Mairi was the light of her heart.

Alex took the letter in exchange for wee Mairi and opened the parchment sealed with the Murray emblem.

"If Jamie has one more joke in here aboot that wee devil Cameron being wedded to our angel Mairi, I will send him my fist," he said humorously, as Jamie loved to tease him about such. "Our Mairi will never, ever wed, and be with us forever."

Grace scoffed and sat down, bouncing Mairi on her lap. "Oh, look at the change fatherhood has made in you! The Highland Heartbreaker is such a prude," she teased.

"Dinnae fash. When we have a son, I will ensure he is nothin' like me as a lad. I now see the error of my ways," he said in an exaggerated brogue, raising his hand in a solemn vow.

"Ye silly man," Grace giggled, imitating his brogue. "Come on and read out the letter already."

"Alex, Grace, and wee Mairi, we hope ye are all well. We send the same well wishes fer dear Kenna, and Nanny too, of course. Regretfully, we have some news, and we implore ye to keep yer ears open fer any information. It appears Duncan is missing."

"Oh, the poor Murrays! And poor Kenna – you know how deeply she feels for Duncan, and she has not seen him since the day we returned from that despicable situation," Grace whispered, pressing her hands over Mairi's ears as she said the last words.

Alex first grinned at her overprotectiveness, but then grimaced at the gravity of the thoughts her words evoked.

"Aye, I ken," he said quietly. He turned his eyes back to the letter and continued reading out loud. "We intend to stop by as I scour the nearby clans fer word and will entrust Izzy, Jennet, and Cameron to ye. See ye soon, old friend."

"The bad news aside, I look forward to their company and the babes will prove a distraction for Kenna. I think we should tell her tonight, as I do not like keeping this from her," Grace said with a sad smile. He loved that about her; she always knew what to say, and knew how to find a light in any darkness.

"Grace, *mo chridhe, mo ghradh*, ye ken I would be nothin' without ye be my side. Ye and my wee Mairi. *Tha gràdh agam ort*," he told her, hearing his voice thicken with emotion as he walked over to the chair where they sat. He crouched down in front of them, and his eyes found Grace. Their shades of blue crashed like waves meeting turbulently in the middle of the sea. Just as fierce was their love.

"There are no words I love more than the words you say to me in Gaelic, my Highland Heartbreaker."

Reader's Note

Thank you, lovely reader for if you are reading this, you enjoyed Highland Heartbreaker to the end.

Aesop's Fables

As I did in *The Bonniest Lass in Scotland*, I have referenced another ancient fable. It fascinates me that these ancient tales, full of morals and wisdom, will forever remain prevalent across any generation. I have no evidence to support a Scottish storyteller who would have told these stories, but what I do know is folklore and storytelling was a very big part of the Scottish tradition, as it was for many ancient and medieval civilisations. Or, I would say for anyone, before the printing press and technology came about!

Heroine with Anxiety and Herbal Remedies

In Grace, I envisioned a character who was strong, like in my first two books. From the very first chapters, Izzy and Charlotte were feisty and unconventional for their respective times. This time, I wanted a different kind of depth. Mental health is topical and something I respect as different to each individual, whether you have or know someone who has experienced such.

For the purpose of my story, and it being set in a specific time period, I steer away from using the term 'anxiety'. The origin of the word 'anxiety' comes from the Latin *angere* ('to choke'). Grace grew up in an unkind home environment that resulted in anxious behaviours. But, when she found support, security, and tools (by way of herbal remedies, that centuries later are still used), she began to see a difference in how she would respond when she perceived a threat or hostile situation. And again, anxiety is unique to everyone, and the fictional circumstances of Grace coming to navigate her anxiety and fight her fears may seem unrealistic but are based on personal experience and research.

About the Author

Forever reading, forever dreaming. And mainly, forever wishing I was dancing at a Regency Ball, drinking whisky in a medieval Scottish keep, navigating a Norman-Saxon romance, or riding up on horseback into a Western town.

Follow my writing journey, as one by one these stories will unfold.

To be kept informed of new releases, updates, and most importantly to connect with any feedback or reviews, please see my Linktree: https://linktr.ee/SteffySmithBooks for all the options available!

As an indie author, I humbly ask you to leave a review on Goodreads, Amazon, Kobo, Kindle, or GooglePlayBooks – whichever platform you use. Or feel free to reach out to me directly. I thank you in advance for your support & truly hope you enjoyed the second instalment of *Highland Hearts ~ Highland Heartbreaker*!

Also by Steffy Smith

A Marquess of Roses

A feisty hoyden. A devilish rake. Step back in time to Regency London.

The ton is ready for another season to start but is the ton ready for Lady Charlotte FitzHugh of Kentwell?

The Marquess of Sunderland, Adam Langdon, will not know what hits him when he sets his emerald eyes upon her amethyst orbs.

Nor will the Lord whose foot she stamps on. Nor the Viscount she knee's in the bollocks.

No shrinking violet is Lady Charlotte, and the Marquess will be unable to resist.

Available in paperback from Amazon

The Bonniest Lass in Scotland

Isobel MacNeil has grown up a simple village Lass and craves adventure, knowledge and love.

Laird Jamie Murray is looking for a woman who will bring a strong alliance and run his keep.

Love is not required.

When the two encounter each other in a loch, her bathing and him grievously wounded, sparks fly, and passions ignite.

Secrets threaten to not only pull them apart but bring them closer together.

But can he accept she has nothing to offer but herself? And can she help him see past the nature of his stubborn ways?

The highlands can be harsh and cruel. When Isobel goes missing their love is put to the test.

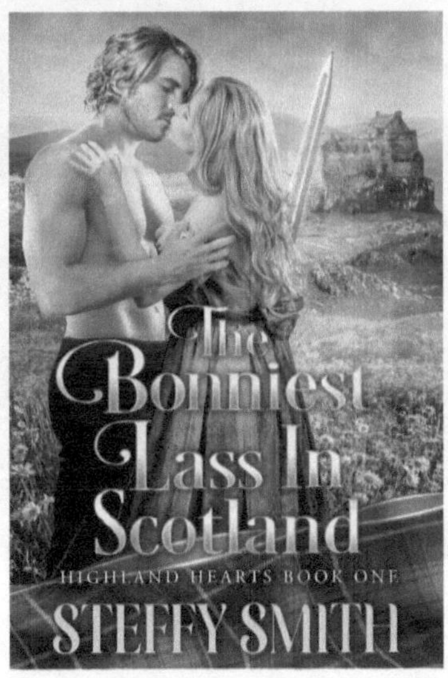

Available in paperback from Amazon